SUICIDE BIBLE

THE STORY OF NATOSHA LITTLE

ANGELO BARNES

 www.trafford.com

North America & international
toll-free: 844-688-6899 (USA & Canada)
fax: 812 355 4082

Acknowledgments

So many have assisted me during the exciting journey of this manuscript. First and foremost, Allah gets the praise. I thank the creator for my beautiful children (Shameia, Angelo, Isaiah, Shiloh, Ishe, and Vision). I couldn't have done it without my beautiful mother and sister (Catherine Barnes and Natasha Barnes). Shot out to my brothers, uncles, nieces, nephews, aunts, and cousins. My grandmother (Maxine Barnes) always been my rock. Antonnita Anthony, thanks for hanging in there with me; that means so much. Jamal Carter and Bobby Barnes are the best cousins ever. My uncles Courtney and Norman, I'll always love them as brothers. Though my sister initially read the story on yellow paper, Avery Little and Andrew Tuell were the first who read the finished version of the manuscript, giving it an awesome rating; both are very close friends of mine. Randy Davis was always there to help take my thoughts to the next level. Leighton Anderson is my walking buddy, never complaining about me talking him to death about writing. Gregory Johnson helped format the cover; he's also one of my closes friends. Romero Ortuna, JR, Wyman Ushry, Alvin Reeves, Dominic Williamson, Ronald White, Martin Leach, Derrick Moore, VA, Nod-Ball, Andrew Compos, JB, Rodney Brooks, James Jones, Debralan Mosley, Denine Mitchell (Thanks for the original version of my cover design), Bikey, Moe, Royal Downs, Zoe, Stink, and Darron Williams all contributed in some fashion, being it heedlessly or knowingly. There are some people who I can't mention; thank you for playing an instrumental role.

Lastly, I'd like to thank Trafford Publishing. Big daps to all my readers.

AN ANGELO BARNES NOVEL

SUICIDE BIBLE: THE STORY of NATOSHA LITTLE

And in her was the blood

of prophets, and of saints,

and of all that were slain

upon the earth.

Revelation 18:24

"The date is April 25, 2006. Time, 11:25 p.m." Christy wrote in silence. While recording facts of the death scene on her pad, she turned towards the rookie patrolman to gather data. "Are you the first responding officer?"

Fresh out of the academy, only securing a few active scenes, Officer Bowles pressed a hankie against his nose. The aggressive scent of rotten flesh was something he refused to get used to. "Yeah, got here 2300 hours."

"Black female," Christy assessed the corpse, pen shadowing every word, "advanced stage of decomposition. It appear she's been simmering for awhile. The remains are indefinable."

"Don't think we'll need much of an ambulance," retorted a plain-clothes officer also on the scene. He was tall with a solid frame, deep tan.

Christy thought maybe he'd been in the oven too long, for his statement was fueled by a bizarre humor that only he himself found funny.

Officer Bowles relayed the info he collected, "Neighbors reported a bad smell coming from this residence, and the female was said to live alone." He handed the detective a Maryland State ID. "They also concluded she haven't been seen in days."

Christy canvassed the identification card. The victim's name was Natosha Little. The moment she was born until now would've made her twenty-three years of age. No need for the deceased to have been camera shy, for she had a beautiful smile. Without a blemish caught by the Department of Motor Vehicle, her complexion was that of a Valentine's Day chocolate. Now the only thing that remained of a natural eye-catcher was an inflated shell. Flower sheets painted rouge indicated both wrists had been sliced. No razor on or near the bed. No blood trail leading from a spot Natosha may have cut her own wrist and staggered back onto the mattress. To an inexperienced gander, it appeared as a suicide, but was she really a victim of foul play?

"I want luminol applied to this bedroom and hallway. We need to know if there's any microscopic blood spatter matching the victim. I also want these sheets submitted to ECU," Christy instructed.

"Ridiculous," said the humor-ridden officer as he joined the detective alongside the bed. "I mean, we don't even know if she's a victim yet. It's clear she killed herself."

"Let's get this straight," contemptuously, Christy's mouth aimed and shot, "when you graduate to Homicide as I have, only then will your opinion get airtime. Since this is my case, hear and obey."

Watching his coworker's face turn pink, Bowles squeezed between the pair to ease tension. He admired how Detective Gatewood took charge as a black woman. White folk, no matter how low the rank, always had to be in control. Being a black man even he knew how difficult it was to take orders from a black woman, especially one on her game. "We know that this is your investigation. Whatever you say will be done," uttered Bowles.

Barely spilling into her late twenties, the detective exhibited a cashew hue. A medium build doled round hips, more than she dared to showcase. A low cut brought out her eyes and lips. Coupled with her physical assets lived a woman with a high IQ, one consistent with the standard prerequisite for any elite field of science. She could have been a superb doctor or lawyer but chose to be a voice for the dead. Ignoring Bowles, Christy continued scolding the white officer until he apologized and left the room.

Her mind never eluded the possibility of Natosha's death being a suicide, but, as she was taught, it was

3

protocol to cover all ends. The next hour was used to weigh context clues, if suicide was the case, regarding why she might have wanted to kill herself. As time flew the rancid stench of decayed flesh attempted to coerce her into believing it didn't exist; so too with the evidence, but she knew the wiser. Christy sketched a diagram of the scene using a stick figure to represent the corpse, rough lines for the bedroom and hallway. Though instinct said something didn't add up, a visual scan of that area revealed nothing irregular or out of whack. The room was dusted for prints, and photos were taken before the coroner zipped the cold body within a black litter.

"Are you ready to have Ms. Little removed?" asked the coroner.

She answered by giving a snooty hand gesture, allowing the man to proceed with the inevitable.

"Looks like my work here is done," Officer Bowles muttered as they watched the body in tow. "So, if you will excuse me-"

"Hold on," she stopped him en route, "just one more question."

He leveled eyes with hers. "Sure... anything."

"How did you get in?" She smiled. "Certainly Natosha

didn't open the door."

"Oh," he returned a chummy simper, "the door was unlocked, but there's a key, maybe a house key, downstairs on the fridge."

She swallowed reluctantly. "I was just wondering."

"No problem."

Chaperoning him as he left the room, she strolled downstairs to the kitchen. And there it was, stuck to a magnet on the refrigerator, the key just as Bowles said. She grabbed it and made it out of the residence just in time to see the last patrol unit dip. Now the detective was alone and that was how she preferred it. All she needed was the automatic holstered beneath her left breast. The gun didn't talk or suggest. It never got in her way nor blew a case due to negligence. A few years back she hated the thing but learned to accept it as another part of the body.

Nosy bystanders stood in the distance. People always wanted something to talk about yet often came down with a case of selective amnesia when questioned by law enforcement. However, Christy caught wind of a weeping woman a few porches over. She walked to the elderly neighbor. "Hello, I'm Detective Gatewood. I take it you knew Natosha?"

Using wrinkled arms to keep her raggedly housecoat intact, the woman asked, "What happened?"

"Too early to tell. So far it looks like a possible suicide."

The old lady shattered in tears. "Dat's just awful. It's gonna be hard on her mom."

Christy probed, "Does her mom live around here?"

"Nah," she struggled to get it together, "but her mother sells Avon. Think I got da card inside my carrying bag."

"Can you get it?"

"Wait right here." The lady anxiously rushed into the house, locking the screen door as if the detective would try to follow her inside.

The community was nice and quiet, a working-class neighborhood on the outskirts of Harford Rd. Awaiting the woman's return, Christy stood on the porch for nearly five minutes. Finally the screen door cracked.

"Sorry it took so long," she presented a miniature brochure, "but chu know how it is when junk piles up."

"I do understand." A settled look and amicable hike of a shoulder expressed empathy as Christy continued to pry, "You recall seeing Natosha with any friends?"

"I never seen her meddle with these hot tramps around here. No boyfriend. She was the church type... just her and that Bible."

"Thank you so much. You've been a great help." Christy reached inside her own purse to hand the woman a business card. "I'd appreciate you give me a call if you hear anything that can assist this investigation."

"Of course."

The detective issued a polite farewell and walked down a tiny flight of concrete steps. She was determined to get to the bottom of Natosha's case.

BOOK TWO

Christy dialed the number on the brochure but didn't get through. After a fifth try she decided to run the digits through the system. A hit traced back to a Danielle Little. Her address listed over west. The hour was too late to knock on her door with bad news. Death may not sleep but people do; therefore, the detective camped at her desk and sifted through clues all night. Soon as day broke she steeled herself to pay Danielle a visit.

A new sun reflected illuminating colors off the silver Grand Marquise. It was Christy's personal vehicle. Company cars came with too much red tape. Working in a whip she owned made the job feel personal, more like a way of life rather than career. She traveled up the long blocks of Fulton Avenue, observing it still congested with an illegal presence. Roaming crackheads and drug dealers painted an embarrassing portrait of hopelessness for that impoverished neighborhood.

After locating the house, she took a fast right on Baker Street and slumped the engine. Christy fastened her pea coat to conceal the shame of yesterday's attire. Scattered dust created unwanted allergies as she got out of the car. Since her occupational guidelines weren't to chase or track down drug dealers, she passed one open-aired drug market without raising a brow. Leave the pushers for the Narcotic Division. She was there on bigger business.

Though major holidays had come and gone, the windows of the address were still decorated with Christmas paraphernalia. Bags of trash, discarded beside a banister, made the front entrance an eyesore. The detective gave the door an assertive knock...

[Clunk! Clunk! Clunk!]

A third-floor window hiked open. Out appeared an apple-head shaped man with bushy hair. Before he could speak, his head was snatched inside and replaced with that of a females. Angrily, she inquired, "Why da hell you knockin' on my door dis time of mornin'! Who you?"

Christy braced herself, putting on a professional face expression. "Ma'am, I'm Detective Gatewood from the Baltimore Homicide Unit. I'm looking for Ms. Little."

The woman uttered with conviction, "Well, I know Ms. Little, but she ain't kilt nobody."

A stubborn cheek tainted Christy's smile. "Never said she did."

Inspecting the visitor's casual rags, all the woman

9

could picture was a debt collector. Since collection agencies been pestering her about hospital bills, gas and electric, she figured this to be the constables' last magic trick to drag her into a courtroom. She stuck to her lines, "I ain't saw Danielle, Ms. Watergate. She outta town."

Christy corrected the mispronunciation of her name, "It's Gatewood, ma'am."

"Ummm-hum, let chu tell it."

Getting nowhere, she gave up. "I'm leaving my card in this mailbox. If you happen to see Ms. Little, tell her give me a call. It's about her daughter, Natosha."

The mention of Natosha changed the woman's whole disposition. "What 'bout Tosha?"

Christy used a first name to create comfort, "Are you Danielle?"

"I'm her," she came clean. "Is Tosha okay?"

"I think it would be better if we talked inside," urged Christy.

"I'll be down, hol'on." Danielle disappeared.

Christy soon heard heavy footsteps along with a barking mutt.

[Ruuf... ruuuf... auu'ruf...]

"Kill dat damn noise," yelled Danielle, knowing its

barks were cries caused by deprivation and animal cruelty.

Christy flashed her badge the second the door eased ajar. "Mind putting the dog away?"

Danielle shooed the pooch. "Oh, don't worry 'bout him. Carlos is just a small dog wit a big mouth. He wouldn't bite a cat. Come in."

Christy wasn't so sure when she accepted the invitation. The two climbed a flight of steps lending to a dense living room area. The space was cluttered and reserved for storage; only two mismatched sofas faced one another. The dog hid under the biggest one.

"Is this your daughter?" The detective gave her the ID.

Danielle was too nervous to sit. "Yeah, dat's my baby."

Same bone structure but a lot heavier, she couldn't help but think about how much Danielle favored the victim. "When is the last time you spoke with or seen her?"

"It been a minute." The mother relived their past spat but kept it locked in. "Why?"

"I'm sorry," Christy paused, truly hating this part of her job, "but your daughter was discovered in bad shape last night. We found Natosha in her home, wrist sliced."

Danielle's eyes got glossy. "Is she in the hospital?"

The detective looked away, saying as softly as she could, "No... the morgue."

"Lord Jesus." The mother nearly collasped.

Christy helped her to the sofa before continuing, "An autopsy will determine exactly when and how she passed. Suicide might be the cause."

First came a moan, then a loud wail that shook the house. A man flew down the steps to Danielle's aid. He was the same dude from the window. An aggressive liquor stench invaded the air as he wrapped his arms around Danielle and asked, "What's wrong, woman?"

"It's Tosha. She killed herself."

Holding back his own tears, he grimaced in utter disbelief.

Momentarily becoming another piece of furniture, Christy stood still and watched. A bunch of questions came that she couldn't answer. Trying to comfort the family, she could only say, "I'm the leading detective handling your daughter's case. There are some discrepancies that I can't speak on while this matter is under investigation. I'll sort this out. If I find there's a perpetrator, they will be brought to justice."

The guy spent the next few minutes speaking on how Natosha was this spiritual giant, recalling weeks when she confined herself in a room to study God's word. Hurt made him stare downward as if his eyes belonged to the floor, "When I asked her 'bout what she been studying, the crusader gave me ah drawn out speech 'bout how salvation was personal, and if one is in search of truth, he must pick up his own cross."

Between sniffles, the mother briefly reminisced, "Yes, my baby was one of a kind. Leavin' dat Bible was like leavin' God behind."

Feeling their pain, a newly mended bond was shared amid the three. To be used as an instrument of hope, depended upon to enforce retribution, both fed Christy's motivation to strive as if every victim was one of her own relatives. Balancing lopsided scales was her way in making a difference in the world. She partook in a group hug, leaving a portion of her own heart behind. Danielle was encouraged to keep in touch.

Christy made it back to her vehicle with haste, tuning the radio station into Heaven 600. As the blessed vocals of an unfamiliar gospel song flooded the car, she shook off the gravity of sorrow and pulled away.

BOOK THREE

"It's a few things in life you must know," Raymond told his daughter over pizza. "Sweetheart, you can't have a rose without thorns. This world is twofold, good or bad. Never get stuck in the middle. Choose the right side and you'll prosper. It's as simple as that."

As both were seated in a pavilion at the Inner Harbor, Christy soaked up her dad's words as if they were from God Almighty. Daddy was all she had after the heated divorce and prolonged custody battle between he and her mom, Christina. The standoff ended with mom getting the house and car; dad walked away with a broken heart and a preteen.

The earnings from his occupation, as a lieutenant within homicide, went toward alimony and living expenses. In catering to the long shifts that Raymond's job required, the obligation of being a single parent became more like a partnership between the two. Christy understood at times she would have to govern herself. Each day was clockwork seeing her off to school and getting home in time to plant a good-night kiss, throw in a microwave dinner, and prepare for his next day. Therefore, whenever they got an opportunity to have a moment out on the town, it was the best to Christy.

Raymond took pride in rewarding his child for the smallest of things. As a matter-of-fact, their journey to the Inner Harbor was one of those examples in thanking Christy for doing so well in school. "You're a special young lady. You'll be someone big who will make a difference in this world. You might be the first female president... I just know it," said Raymond, rubbing his fingers through her hair.

That's the dad she remembered. He was her hero before the drinking came into play. The introduction into alcoholism didn't come with caution, the sudden change came all at once. As work hours got longer, patience got shorter. He and Christy went from maintaining a great relationship to barely speaking. The more Raymond reduced himself to a message in the bottle, the more Christy concealed pain by sticking her head further into the books. The day after graduation, which fell on her eighteenth birthday, a shooting at a gas station left one off-duty lieutenant dead. What started as an exchange of words ended with three shots. Sore from her dad's death, Christy joined the academy six months later. Though the suspect was

15

ultimately caught, tried, and convicted, Raymond was never revived back to the living.

Just as with school, Christy graduated from the academy with honors. She was now a second-generation police officer and took it to heart. Rewarded with a badge and a post on Pennsylvania Avenue, soon the fragrance of an outstanding work ethic reached the nostrils of her superiors. It was naturally in Christy's genes to be a company girl.

She frequently heard stories about how her dad was a marvellous detective and how his misfortune devastated the whole department. Sympathy merged with hard work, wearing Raymond's last name as a charm, helped Christy quickly climb the ranks. She rose from Patrol to plain-clothes, working Burglary until becoming a detective in the Robbery Division. Back then she was twenty-four. After stuffing half of Baltimore's pillagers under the jail, at twenty-eight she transferred to Homicide. The department seen it as her destiny to walk in her father's shoes.

* * * *

Glancing at the many strip clubs and food spots, Christy drove through The Block. The Grand Marquise passed

Gay Street and nailed a left into Central Headquarters. She whipped through the garage and took the parking space of another unmarked vehicle. The top floor had only a few cars, which indicated that the rest of Christy's five-man squadron were out on call. She lamped in her car pondering the Natosha Little's case, unsure if it was even a case at all.

When she finally bounced from the car, the elevator was there as if it had been awaiting her. The detective entered the small mechanical box and pressed the sixth floor. As the elevator reached its destination, the door slid open to the sector sergeant, Neal. He was a fat man with a stubble cut.

"I'm looking for you, Gatewood." He gestured his head with a nudge. "Follow me."

How convenient was it to run into the last person Christy wanted to see. Being personally escorted either meant she was about to get a pat on the back or a paddle to the ass. In under a minute, mumbling under her breath, she closed his office door and posed in place, asking in a perplexed tone, "Is there a problem?"

"Damn right," exclaimed Sgt. Neal, having Christy in the same position Raymond had him in fifteen years earlier.

"The captain chewed my tusk concerning you."

"Oh, I just placed my vehicle in that parking spot for a second," she lied, assuming that was his reason for the conference.

"No, that's not why I chased you down. I wash it was just that simple."

She sensed anger and discomfort in his demeanor. "Then what is it?"

His voice climbed a pitch, "My God... when is the last time you closed a case? You currently have two dozen open files as primary investigator, another twenty or so as secondary. You've let high profile cases slip through your fingers. I've been keeping you out of a shoal, but I can't for much longer."

This was more than a spanking. "I don't need you breathing down my back. That will only make me feel boxed in; I need space to work."

Instead of scratching his head, he shifted and adjoined both hands on his belt. "All I've done is cover for you. The captain is beginning to believe Homicide might not be your pluck."

"Excuse me," she muttered with attitude. "Let's discuss all the cases I did close."

Sgt. Neal placed a firm grip on her shoulder. "See, kiddo," he looked her in the eyes with an expression of concern and wisdom, "this department is like writing a book or making a song. No matter how amazing your project turns out, you're only as good as your last hit."

"I appreciate what you've done for me, gracias, but the captain needs to understand the streets aren't the way they used to be when he walked the beat. Back then people cooperated. Nowadays, those same folks don't want to talk for fear of retaliation. I can't get water out of a rock. I'm doing my best out there."

He couldn't resist picking at his chin. "I'm not saying you aren't dedicated, but this field demands more than a clock burner. Your father knew that and closed more cases by mistake than most detectives did on purpose."

She became annoyed thinking of how her father wasn't so perfect. "I'm not him-"

"But you got him in your blood. Step it up."

Her neck stiffened with pride. "Thought I was."

Sgt. Neal gave stern advice as he showed her to the door, "Get out of your head and get into the mind of your victims. Each homicide is a game of chess. Don't fall in love with the board. Sometimes you must sacrifice the queen to protect the king. I'm not requesting you arrest an innocent citizen, but focus on the pieces and make the right move."

The detective shook her head in agreement but then came more...

"And if you don't close some cases soon," he squinted at his watch as if he couldn't tell time, "I'll be forced to bump you down. You've run out of lifelines."

The door slammed in her face.

When her father was sergeant, Neal was a detective on his squad. Being that her father taught the man all he knew, she expected big favors. Nevertheless, his words held weight, but what more could the department expect when they had one detective doing the work of ten. And as the only female detective on the squad, the rest had tried to work her in a hole, often taking the least difficult cases and leaving her dead ends. It was a male chauvinistic game, and outworking them was her only method of keeping up. "A *true detective*," her father once said, "*is like a doctor, always on call. He is the servant of the people and not a pay check.*"

In her cubical at headquarters, nursing a mug of tea, Christy studied the inconsistencies concerning her present case. So far she didn't have a motive. Was the clue to Natosha's death right before her eyes? Christy took the door key out of her pocket and wondered how she missed it. What else did she overlook? A hunch directed her back to Natosha's home.

BOOK FOUR

Yellow tape, plastic strips that shielded Natosha's home from neighborhood tourism, now whiffled in the breeze. For observational purposes, the detective sat with her engine off until the car absorbed a chill. Two minutes later she looked back at the Grand Marquise from Natosha's porch. Slipping the key into the lock was like turning an ignition, its position shifted with ease. Why hadn't she submitted the key was the million dollar question. Maybe a different set of prints could still be lifted. She'd cross that bridge later.

The residence owned a stinky odor of death. The unpleasant scent deterred the urge of hunger Christy had before entering. She cracked a kitchen window to air out the place. Latex gloves and a small roll of trash bags were removed from her purse. Being extra careful as she recovered items, beginning with the magnet on the refrigerator, she tore apart the downstairs and the second floor. While prying through Natosha's belongings, Christy envisioned if she was demoted how it wouldn't only be counter productive but also defame her father's name. She was in need of a hit. Not just any hit but one very high in profile. If she was fortunate to make a slam dunk, Christy promised not to share that victory with a secondary investigator. At this point success was a necessity she needed, something to represent competency and show her worthy to swing a bat in the major leagues.

Christy felt desperate backtracking an apparent suicide scene, but she had to dig deep. Searching the master bedroom helped her remember what Danielle and the neighbor mentioned about how Natosha feasted on the word of God. Then it gelled. "If Natosha was so spiritual, where's her Bible?" she spoke aloud.

Since the victim was found in her bed, the Bible had to be close. If nothing else she wanted to return the book to Danielle. Noble actions were known to provide a sense of closure. The detective got on one knee and looked under the bed, no book. She lifted the mattress and there it was, a King James bright as day.

As she snatched the Bible and allowed the mattress to reunite with the box spring, its contents fell onto the floor. Christy immediately toiled to recover the sacred script. She arranged the papers into a neat pile and realized it wasn't scripture. The discovery was a diary of some sort. Once the papers were placed in order, Christy got nosy:

Okay, must be gone if you readin' dis. Had you touched dis book while I was on earth, probably would'a cut off ya fingers and rammed them up dat poopa. Yup, you expected da open nis Bible and see Genesis. Forget Adam and Eve, Cain and Able, Noah or da rest of those saints who been dead foreva. Can't help you. If love was da savior of the world then why ain't we rescued? Dats just anotha lie like people thinked dey knew da true me. Imagine nat. Halos and harlots. Peep a piece of my childhood...

The detective was curious as to what followed. How wild was this so-called church girl. She continued reading:

Might'a been ten or eleven when we lived in da Flag House projects. In my era white people knocked on our door every Saturday after cartoons. Dey was from da church but only came in da daytime, smart enough ta not show face at night. No god could protect them in my neighborhood at thos hours. Da nighttime was when I heard da mos shots. Dis white bunch didn't carry guns,

24

just da Bible and big guts. Dey was sponsored by a church out da county. Not one of us was receptive when dey begged da youth ta hit da local recreation center and adhere ta da word of God. Since pleas couldn't do it, dey gave out soft bread and sweet buns. Dat's when most kids in da hood became children of God.

Me and Rose, my besty, went down da recreation center ta sing, stomp, and shout. Must thought we lost our mind. Taught us lots of church hymns different from da rap ova boomboxes. Mrs. Mary made me her personal black project, crammin' me wit homework out da Bible. Gave me one crispy dollar per lesson. Used dat money ta clean out da penny candy store. It turned me ta a Bible mascot, a shinnin' example of what other children could become. Thinked Rose's mova had somedin against white people. Smiled in their face den call dem devils later.

Mommy didn't discriminate. Da Bible program gave us free bread and me somedin da do on weekends. People seen change in me, not dat I was a bad girl. After a few months of missionary work, Mrs. Mary convinced da church ta invest in a cheese bus ta commute all da children who wanted ta attend Sunday service. Da voyage was twenty minutes and free of charge. But da actual church didn't give out buns so da kids stopped goin', even Rose. I continued. Mommy was supportive. Gave her more time wit Mr. Paul.

Sometimes Mrs. Mary would bring me home when treated ta dinner after service. She had a funny shape, no hips, a lot of cardboard. Pretty legs and a God fearin' tude made her stand out. Mrs. Mary's husband worked at some air base and was neva home. Only met him once. I had no brothers or sisters. Mrs. Mary was barren. She took me places and labeled me her biological daughter. Those white people made mockery, but she cared less. It was all 'bout walkin' in da Lord.

Da few times mommy let me stay da weekend we had Bible study all night. Morning she made breakfast and let me run along da community playground. When I didn't want ta go there, I'd stay in na house pickin' wit Richard, her cat. Once... when me and him was alone, think Mrs. Mary was at da car fa somedin, I marveled over his cream and gold fur. Prettiest puss I eva seen. Thing was he been 'round so long dat amnesia kicked in. One minute we friends, next I'm prey, especially when his white queen was out of sight. He get in attack mode and chase me 'round na house.

No body knew 'bout Richard's bipolar, psychopathic episodes but me. So tired of da flea bag, took matters into my own hands dat day. Richard hit da corner wit Lucifer in his eyes, nails out, ready to put in work. Knocked him silly by sayin', "You look hungry. Why don't we go into da kitchen and get a snack."

Swear he licked his lips and preformed some insane attack ritual off da carpet and walls. Scared me all da way ta da refrigerator. Best thing he went fa da bait. Richard suddenly tuned one ear ta a noise picked up by his sixth sense, turning back friendly as if he and me was playmates. "Very catty. Oh, think you heard massa, huh," I said while escortin' him inside da icebox.

Out came a meow, den da tiger. When he leapt ta put a beauty mark on my face, slammed his neck between da refrigerator door. Let it go Richard twitched den fainted. Wasn't breathing when I checked, so I panicked and put him in da freezer. Perfect timin' 'cause Mrs. Mary walked right in da house. I rushed and grabbed my Bible.

"You're just a little angel, aren't you," said Mrs. Mary and gave out goodies.

After readin' a few verses, she gathered my stuff and drove me home. Neva came back 'round.

Christy turned and unholstered her service weapon, pointing it almost aimlessly.

"Hold up! Don't shoot!" shouted Officer Bowles. He was barely through the bedroom door.

Matching the voice with the face, Christy inhaled. "Almost blew you away. What are you doing here?" she asked, tucking the gun and cuffing the Bible.

He had to catch his own breath. "I gave some neighbors my card last night and just received an anonymous tip a strange person came into this house. Surprised to see you."

"Left some clues behind."

"Like that key." He laughed.

"Yeah," she retorted, "guess I'm the one who left the door unlocked this time."

He read into the rhetorical statement as intended. "Definitely, how else would I've gotten in?"

Christy thought it came out wrong but giggled, leaning forward to scoop up plastic bags. "Help take some of this evidence to the car."

"Sure." He noticed the book in her right hand. "Fine time to read the Bible."

She gave him the bags, shrugging, "Just something I keep close. Never know when you'll need God."

She made a good point. "Look like you need a meal and a bath."

He couldn't have been more accurate. Something was different about him. Her eyes scouted the officer from head to toe. The polyester was missing and he looked damn good. Bowles performing a public service, off the clock, said a lot about his character.

"Can tell you had a rough night. I'll take this stuff down headquarters if you like."

His invite was thoughtful, but pride restricted her from bending. "No thanks. I'll be fine."

"Just trying to help," he said, toting the take.

She led the way out of the house. Before they left the porch the front door was double checked. At the trunk Christy dropped the house key in another bag tagged evidence. "Super appreciative. You came in handy."

He palmed her hand instead of accepting a shake. "Hey, let's have coffee tomorrow."

Her mind had five seconds to register his request. Gently withdrawing, Christy told the officer she would have to sleep on it.

Searching her eyes for a soft spot, he replied, "Knew you'd say that, but here's my number."

BOOK FIVE

The evidence was a quick delivery to the fifth floor at headquarters. Soon as it was submitted for analysis, Christy left the building as fast as she walked in. The Grand Marquise took I-93 to Druid Hill Avenue and shot through Park Heights. It wasn't the shortest route but the safest. She knew that area like the back of her hand and could outmaneuver a tail with no problem. Alert as always when driving to the den, a skilled turn penetrated Slade Avenue. Passing the tennis court triggered images of her dad. He wasn't a tennis player but a loyal fan. She worked herself into a migraine whenever trying to troubleshoot his reason for descending into the abyss. She couldn't understand it, probably never would.

Christy weaved a bend and found herself distracted by a family of four at the intersection. A Jewish husband and wife crossed a street holding two toddlers. The children looked so much like twins. Christy desired a family but not until she got married. She went a while twenty-eight years without exposing herself to a man and planned to go twenty-eight more if need be. Christy's lack of romance was part of what kept her career oriented. Now in the process of a potential demotion, a husband was the last topic on her mind.

Thoughts changed with the green light, brain skipping to the words Natosha wrote. It appeared as a mere journal of the girl's life, but facts of life could also contain the mystery behind her death. Natosha didn't come off as a religious junky, but who was Christy to judge. It would be best to read more before jumping to conclusions.

She finally arrived at the complex. Entertaining the same bad habit since a teen, the car was left unlocked. She hit the mailbox at the entrance of her building. More bills in her father's name. They resided in the third floor apartment since the day the courts granted him custody. Christy maintained the two bedroom efficiency even after his death. It was once full of life; now her den was a lonely place. It didn't give hugs or feedback. The walls only listened. Christy entered the apartment with a thought of upgrading, same thought every time before reaching family photos. The option of moving never stuck. This was her home, a vault which contained precious childhood memories.

Her workbag and bulletproof vest went on a hook near the hallway. The gun and diary went with her to the tub.

There she ran hot water and undressed. Nothing surrounding her mattered. Life would resume after she soaked in soothing bath beads. The water rose with attitude as she lowered herself into the tub. Following seven minutes of deep meditation, she grabbed Natosha's Bible:

Ta day mommy smacked me fa pissin' na bed. Said I betta stay in da Bible 'cause ain't no guy gon want a pissy coot.

[Yah triflin' lil heifer!]

See, dats her screamin' now. Sometime wish somedin bad happened ta her. Like what happened ta Richard. Wouldn't be able ta hit me no more.

[Tosha, get cho ass in here!]

Hey, mommy callin'. Got ta go.

Christy identified with Natosha's plight. She used to be a soaker as well, but that came to a halt once dreams were separated from reality. However, dry or wet, she never received a spanking. Christy turned to the next page:

"Shouldn't be kissin' no boy," told Rose's cousin, Lester, but got ignored.

"Kissing won't hurt," he said, settin' next ta me. "Hold your lips out like you blowing ah bubble. I'll do the rest."

Dat boy was persistent. "Mommy said girls get pregnant dat way," told him.

Lester made fun. "What cho momma smokin'? Never seen no girl get pregnant from kissing."

Felt dumb on da inside. Had no business in Rose's bedroom wit him anywhoz. Rose wasn't home, neither was Ms. Stacy. Mommy sent me ova next door da beg fa sugar. Lester tricked me ta da bedroom. He was a monkey. Looked like one, acted like one. Only his chin had hair. "We need sugar, dats it," told him.

"Got some sugar for you alright," was his response.

He worked his hot eyes down my shirt ta my private area. Lied when I felt trouble. "My mova gon blow da spot. She'll come lookin' fa me any second. Give me da sugar and I'll come back."

He said okay but didn't move. Thought den spoke, "Only under one condition."

"What condition?" I was confused.

"Give me the kiss as ah down payment."

His mouth was funky wit crooked teeth. Wasn't gon let me go

til I gave in. So I did. "Okay, but chu gotta peck me once, real fast like a bird."

"You won't even feel it," he promised. "But close your eyes. Act like you dropped something. We'll pretend I bent down to get it and you rewarded me with ah kiss. Let's start off at the kiss part though," Lester anxiously directed.

Wantin' it ova, I closed my eyes, pokin' out my lips.

[Pow!]

Slapped da hell outta me. Seen red stars den grabbed my face.

"Knew you was ah little freak! Just wanted to see what Christ-Girl was going to do," he shouted wit spit flyin' on me.

Couldn't believe he hit me. Got me good, too.

"Better not cry or I'm telling Ms. Danielle you was over here being fresh," he threatened.

No tears fell. Went from holdin' my face ta coverin' my eyes from embarrassment.

"All that God stuff you be into and you over here about to kiss ah boy. Ah hypocrite!"

Dats when Lester gave me da boot. Bad thing mommy also manhandled me fa takin' so long. Plus was empty-handed.

Compassion settled in her heart for Natosha. That was a rough experience for a young girl to endure. The story had Christy stuck:

Lester made my first experience negative wit da opposite sex. Hated boys after dat, even da ones in my class. Stepped into a big challenge in elementary and middle school. Mommy neva got me name brand clothes 'cause I wasn't there ta participate in a ghetto fashion show. Dat's what she said. Sick of her sayin' school was an institution of higher learnin', but she neva let me go. If her doctor's appointment called fa my company, which dey always did, school was placed on na back burner. Grocery shoppin', house cleanin', and trips ta social service all meant another absence on my report card.

When I finally made it ta school, my presence threw off da vibe of da class. Whispers and snickers surrounded my sneakers. Dey laughed at Meka and Kevin, too. Looked like our moms shopped at da same Goodwill. Though me, Meka, and Kevin had da sameding in common, dey acted like dey was betta den me. Da Lord's holy gift ta humanity. Least we could'a ate dagather at lunch.

Neva happened. It was always just me and my bible.

Middle school was different. Stayin' ta myself saved me from gettin' boxed in. Classmates thought I had a mental illness. Dey just feared da unknown. God spoke ta dem through me. Still seen their motives, wolves in na sheep jerkin, serpents. Stead of stayin' clear of snakes, learnt ta pick up da most venomous kinds wit da agent of kindness. Call dat a miracle...

"Go head, say something to her," some dude told his friend in na aisle across.

Was in 7eleven makin' my usual rounds before first period. Addicted ta chilli and cheese hot dogs. Frequented dat spot ta da point of becomin' a regular, which made it more easy ta cop a dog and steal a cake. Neva knew what hit dem.

"Excuse me, shorty," da boy stepped closer, blockin' da middle aisle, "my homeboy think you cute and wanna know if he can say hello?"

He zeroed in on my busted shoes. Tell he tried to hold back his laughter. Since his approach wasn't sincere, put a picture of da invisible man in my mind, and walked pass him like da two wasn't even there. Besides, my bookbag was filled wit a lion's share of pastrys. Dem sweets went home *wit me. Da dumb boys didn't.*

Christy closed the book as her eyes fell victim to gravity. The story was interesting enough to pick up later. She pulled the plug out of the drain and reached for a towel as the cold water escaped. The hygienic practice of rinsing soap off the body only happened when she pampered herself. Tonight wasn't one of those occasions. Dabbing the cotton fabric over her pores, she rummaged through a cosmetic basket posted between the toilet and sink. Locating one of her just-in-case tampons, Christy gradually inserted the feminine article into her moist cavity. It was better to be safe than sorry.

Suddenly a pang of household errands ate at her. Everyday chores such as cleaning dishes, washing clothes, taking out trash, and other domestic duties were neglected due to a lack of downtime. But her messy apartment didn't have to suffer from the judgemental opinions of spectators. No one was ever invited inside. In fact, her dad was the last man, so much so that even his room remained the same way he left it. Being raised not to tinker with his property, she couldn't recall the last time that door had been open.

Tucked within the garret of her imagination existed a yearning, one crippled by the reality that her father wasn't coming back home. No wrong could be righted between them. Same story with Natosha, even with Raymond and his extensive list of earthly accomplishments, both were reduced to just a file. Her way to keep Raymond's legacy alive was to find apiece of him in every homicide she worked. Every case was converted into a single puzzle piece. The more cases Christy solved, she reasoned, the more the puzzle of her shattered heart would come together. She planned to donate more of self, anything to make her dad proud.

Christy spent the rest of her night catching up on needed sleep.

BOOK SIX

After picking up her son from the sitter, Linda noticed the presence of a patrol car but tried to think nothing of it. A mile up the road the young mother was nervous when her Buick got pulled to the side of the Baltimore Cemetery. It felt weird and uncomfortable. She asked from behind the wheel, "Can you tell me why I've been stopped?"

"No." The flashlight shined in her face. "Step out."

His bright light was like having the whole moon in her car. To avoid blindness, Linda peered at her sleeping infant in the back seat. "This is a waste of time," she uttered before complying.

The driver was short with a voluptuous backside. He pressed her against the hood. "Got any drugs or weapons on you that I need to know about?"

Discombobulated as his hands cunningly massaged her breast, she immediately felt violated. "Watch your paws!"

Without one motorist in sight, he continued his lewd shakedown.

"Excuse me," Linda resisted, "shouldn't I be getting searched by a female officer?"

The lights of an oncoming vehicle broke his spell.
"Shut up, lest you wanna make commissary for interfering
with an officer's duty."

She shuttered but stood firm.

He turned her to face him. "Watched you ignore a stop
sign five blocks back. Ran your tags and they're not a
match for this Buick."

That was impossible. The car and title was in her name.
Had the officer mentioned her driving without insurance,
he'd been on point. Sharing the wrong information proved he
didn't truly read her tags. She mentally recorded the name
on his uniform. "That's a lie. These tags are mine. You
must of punched something in wrong."

He scanned her peach skin, dying to find a second
reason to grope her. "You're lucky tonight. No need to be
sassy. Don't turn an anthill into a mountain. Learn your
lesson and keep it moving."

What lesson was there to get out of being pulled over
by a cop and touched inappropriately. *Owings* was the name
she promised to report to a higher authority. "You're out
of your mind. I don't deserve this harassment. Y'all pigs
are a trip."

The officer wasn't about to tolerate the fatlip. "Look,

since you want to be a cunt, give me your license. I'm writing you a ticket."

That didn't sound so bad. She could use the ticket as proof he pulled her over. "Write until your fingers fall off. Make sure you spell my name correctly."

As she bent over to retrieve the card from the cup holder, he studied her spread and thought how an ass like that needed to be explored.

Linda sensed him beaming and didn't have to look back to picture his face. The officer's physical features were basic: Brown skin, fat nose, big lips, clean cut. How could she forget it. "Here, take the license."

[Ssswop.]

The woman would pay later for forcefully slapping the card in his hand. "Wait in your vehicle until I get back," he said, emotionless.

Though in a combative state, she obeyed his order.

He wasn't really writing a ticket. Her information was what he desired. In seconds her name and address were scribbled down and stashed behind his sun visor.

Linda looked back at the patrol vehicle through her side mirror. The Baltimore Police Department would be sued for Owings' sexual assault. She wouldn't be dissuaded from seeking justice. The event was despicable, an outright insult on her integrity as a mother, woman, and nurse.

The officer walked back to the Buick. "Ms. Linda Foreman."

"What?"

"You're right. Reran your information," he dropped the license in the car near her vagina, "and you came back clean. Sorry, I was wrong."

She felt used and abused. "You rotten sonofabitch."

The officer took her yap only because the stop was a hoax; he knew it, so did she. "Thank you for your cooperation. Drive safe. Watch those signs."

The deceptive gleam in his eyes made Linda queasy. As he turned to stroll, the woman called him every name in the book before peeling off.

He nibbled on the sweet taste of victory, promising to nail it the next time. Unbuttoning the bogus name tag on his uniform, Officer Bowles replaced it with his own. It was impossible to report an officer who didn't exist. He would see Linda again. Saucy girls like her needed to be taught a lesson.

BOOK SEVEN

When the alarm clock blasted a static love song, Christy hauled herself out of comfort to brave the challenge of a new workday. Scrubbing her face and teeth was the first hump, deciding what to wear was the second. A pair of fitted jeans, some jogging shoes, and a buttermilk blouse was nominated. Her holster strap was concealed under a stonewashed jacket. A swift breeze of determination confirmed the possibility of making it to work on time.

Within fifteen minutes the Grand Marquise glided into a prohibited parking space at headquarters. The department preferred quality over numbers. Win more with less; everyone had to carry their own weight. Though rough cases placed her at the bottom of the totem pole, a demotion was hogwash. What about the files she closed like Tonya Gibbs; that case involved the rape and murder of a nine-year-old whose junky mother handed her to local drug dealers to cover a debt, or how about sixteen-year-old Courtney Mars who fatally shot his parents as the result of being grounded. Her superiors must have forgotten about Boncelle Dickens who poisoned her husband in an attempt to cash in on his life insurance.

Christy's list of victories went on. So many issues attacked her mind from the car to the elevator.

"Hey, Gatewood," a voice called out.

She obliged with a no-nonsense twist of the neck.

Detective Miles and his partner, Chance, approached from a distance. They were the playboys of the squad. Miles was a slim guy who gave new meaning to the word ugly. He favored a cricket in suit and tie. On the other hand, Chance was built like a thumb, possessing a face only a mother could love. Despite their odd appearances, both worked together so well that one could start a sentence and have the other finish it. Every case they touched was closed in forty-eight hours.

Christy turned back towards the elevator as it opened. Three got off, and she got on.

"Hold that square," shouted Miles, speeding with his shadow, Chance.

She understood the job was a place of business and not a platform to express personal dislikes. Though she didn't do the James Brown at the initial sound of Chance calling her, it was out of character to be rude and unprofessional. So the door was held out of common courtesy, but she'd rather seen it close in their faces.

"Heard me enough to hold the elevator, not enough when I called your name. What's your deal?" Chance asked in a light monotone.

Christy's persona was nonchalant. "Should I have bent over backwards?"

"And fish the place out... no thanks," chimed Miles, sarcastically.

"Look, girls," Christy folded her arms as the arch of her right foot danced about the heel, "find someone else to spar with. I'm not the one."

Through clinched teeth, Chance uttered like a ventriloquist, "Don't hate, congratulate."

She ignored Chance and addressed Miles, "Will you get your hand out of your partner's ass."

Miles sneered as if her comeback was inappropriate.

Before Chance could cock and pop, Christy held up a hand to signify that enough was enough. Once the door opened, she was the first to exit. Her feet found the squad room where officers lolled with coffee in hand, all absorbing the words of Capt. Dagger. He was albino. Fuzzy brows and a pointed nose made his butt chin acceptable. The force respected him as a man of action. When he spoke, people listened.

"Seriously," the captain concluded, "we smile to keep from crying. But nothing is funny when somebody son, mother, father, sister, brother, aunt, uncle, cousin, or baby is laying across a gurney. The community is depending on us, and we can't let them down. So get out there today and find some suspects, close some cases, and make some arrests!"

Christy felt a tap on the shoulder and there stood Sgt. Neal.

"Follow me, Gatewood," he whispered and walked off.

She hoofed it to a hallway just a couple of doors short of his office. Staring at her as if yearning to say something he'd later regret, she tried to break the monotony with the first thing that came to mind, "Some speech by Capt. Dagger, huh?"

"Heard it all before." He handed Christy a piece of paper. "Here's an address. A call just came in that might be helpful to you."

It was a house on the 3100 block of Lawnview Avenue. The location was around Belair Road. That part of the city haunted her with unpleasant memories, especially since it was the last area her father was seen alive.

"Time adds to the disintegration of a crime scene. Get

47

"Danielle, a man in all black ran from your daughter's house about an hour ago. I started to call that lady who gave me her card yesterday."

She entertained the fibbing neighbor up until that point. "What lady?" asked Danielle.

"Think her name was Christina or something. I still got the card if you want it..."

It took every fiber within her being not to slam the door in the neighbor's face. Danielle may have believed Brenda if she and Paul hadn't been in Natosha's home for well over sixty minutes. "No, Brenda. I'm good. Keep your card."

The lady tried to peer through the cracked door. "Just thought it best to let y'all know what I saw."

It was clear that Ms. Brenda was snooping around. Danielle kindly thanked her and eased the door closed. "What is wrong wit these people," said Danielle as she violently stomped past Paul in the dinning room, "lose a child and they still won't let you hurt in peace."

He wore a confused look. "Dat lady don't know what she talking 'bout."

Natosha was like a daughter to Paul. He been around since she was a little girl. Her father jumped ship, so he carried the load. Paul was known as a flat-foot hustler who panhandled, pawned jewelry, and made the blood bank his second home. He felt less than a man for not having a respectable, steady occupation. Though he begged and borrowed, Paul never broke law. That principle alone kept him afloat.

On the other side of the coin, thriving off of a fixed income, welfare was the signature trademark of Danielle's family for generations. Since her daughter's graduation from high school, social service cut Natosha from her check. She was proud of Natosha being the first in the family to finish school, but breaking a generational curse didn't contribute to financial obligations. Welfare worked for Danielle, and she wouldn't see it no other way.

Natosha was one who never accepted poverty. She didn't let it place her at a disadvantage. Determined to find work, she landed a job doing door-to-door sales. Grant Marketing began as a fun adventure, promoting a promise that Natosha could open her own business in a year. Until then her earnings were based on commission. The job came with long hours, no benefits, no 401K. Her income was

predicated on luck and a strenuous work effort. The
challenge ultimately tore at Natosha's endurance, causing
her to vacate the job.

After living life on a false promise, Natosha decided
to search for a stable career. Once accepted for Financial
Aid, she took up Mortuary Science. It was only a two year
course. But when she found herself in the presence of a
dismembered infant, the poor girl ejected her stomach
lining all over the deceased child. It took months to void
herself of that gross image, and she would have completed
the course if only the nightmares subsided. Natosha found
another job at a candle shop, and that's what she stuck
with.

"Bump Brenda," Danielle's tone was uneasy, "help me
with these valuables so we can get out of here."

"Woman, you the one standing there like ah statue. I'm
ready," said Paul.

"Then come on." She pulled at his arm.

To Danielle valuables were items such as baby pictures
and knickknacks. Paul followed his mate as she explored
each room, taking down curtains, going through linen, and
wrapping lamps. Using public transportation limited her
take. Danielle left the house thinking about the last

conversation she and Natosha had...

"Can't always depend on me. I got bills also," Natosha huffed into the receiver.

"Stop cryin' broke. Shouldn't be in dat big house alone, anywhoz. If you come back home, da other room is yours. It'll give you all da privacy you need," Danielle explained for her own selfish reasons.

Natosha got agitated. "Ma, you only thinkin' 'bout yourself. Want me back home so dat I can help you wit bills."

Danielle's attitude got the best of her. "How dare you challenge me when I'm only tryin' to help out. Shove dat money and house right up dat holy ass of yours. I don't need-"

The phone went dead.

"Hello. Hello," said the mother before realizing she got boothed on.

That was the final straw that made them both call it quits.

BOOK NINE

The setting was like unto a scene from C.S.I. where the trajectory of emergency lights reflected off of windows and porches. Three marked vehicles blocked the one-way street. As Christy double-parked, two women lamented while conversing with an officer. The females were either close friends or relatives of the victim. Beyond the caution tape, as with any other scene, spectators eye-balled the action. The detective traipsed through the minor commotion, making her initial appearance inside the home. The silence of death was hidden behind foot traffic and loud walkie-talkies. She was suddenly taken by the busy atmosphere.

"Over here, detective," a middle-aged, dark skinned officer called out as he greeted her scratching his head. He had a round face, heavy bags under the eyes.

"What's the narrative?" asked Christy.

"Ah female apparently committed suicide. She was discovered by her mother and sister."

That stunned her. "Suicide?"

"Yeah, suicide," repeated the officer, convinced such a reality wasn't beyond the realm of human endeavor, at least not for a homicide detective. "I'll escort you to your princess."

Scoping every little detail, Christy followed the officer. The walls and carpet had a creme theme. A huge entertainment system, furniture, and a spectacular array of organic plants occupied a front area. The living room and dining room were in juxtaposition. To the side of the kitchen was a basement door much smaller than the standard code. Its entrance was an unusual portal, urging the pair to lower their heads to avoid injury.

Bewitched by a self-imposing spell, Christy plodded down the wooden flight watching each step leading to the bottom level. Around a sharp corner hung a poorly constructed drop ceiling. Stooping low took them to a makeshift gym. Inside the tiny room was everything from universal workout machines to old-fashioned pig iron. Upon one of the benches lied the victim.

Christy mulled over her pretty peach tone. Both eyes were still cracked in a dreamy state. The life source that once kept her alive now drained through deep gashes in her wrist. Christy's mind instantly made a connection between that woman and Natosha. Though a box cutter was in the victim's left hand, the blade looked clean. The scene was staged.

"Sgt. Neal," Christy uttered with excitement, "I'm sure we have a possible serial killer on the loose, and we must nab this person before someone else gets hurt."

"Slow down, Detective," Sgt. Neal reclined in a leather seat behind his desk, "I can only wonder what stencil you're using to draw this conclusion."

"Okay, look," she copped a squat, "the other day I was called to the residence of a Natosha Little-"

"Tell me something I don't know."

Ignoring his crassness, she spoke on, "Her wrist was cut. No razor or any other sharp object in sight. We sprayed major areas for plasma-"

"Textbook-"

"But I didn't discover any blood around the bed or in the hallway. That raised my antennas."

"Great spider senses," cheered Sgt. Neal. "Carry on."

"According to a neighbor, she had no male or female friends, no motive to take her own life. Then today..."

"Um-hum-"

Christy put her head and shoulders into it, "The victim in that house on Lawnview turned out to be a Linda

Foreman; she was a nurse who interned at University Hospital. The mother and sister said they just spoke with her that evening, agreeing to pick up Linda's infant. The front door was unlocked when they got there. The infant was upstairs in her pen while Linda was in the basement with her wrist sliced open."

"And the child's father?"

"From what I've been told he's incarcerated over City Jail. The beef is armed robbery."

Sgt. Neal paused. "Well, that excludes him."

"Mom says her daughter was a loner, promised she was happy and wouldn't have ended her own life. She had a kid to care for. And even though a box cutter was recovered on the scene, I believe the killer placed it there."

Sgt. Neal knew his opinion would likely leave a scar. "I hear what you're saying, but all I see is two suicide victims, no connection."

"I see it different," she contested. "And I'm sorry if our views conflict."

"You owe me no apology. We're all entitled to our own sentiments."

"Can't you see," Christy's emotions flared, "whoever did this gets off on making the victim look like they've killed themselves. He targets females, introverts, those who live alone."

Sgt. Neal juggled the facts. She made good points. He inwardly agreed that the detective was potentially right, but what if she wasn't. That would crush her career. He witnessed Raymond almost go crazy over a case before he physically departed. Detective Gatewood was the female version of her father, both were like hounds when chasing a lead. The difference between the two was he knew when to let go, his daughter didn't. Perhaps it was desperation that catered to Christy's momentum; no one had a clue. But despite whatever, Raymond was one of Sgt. Neal's comrades, and it wasn't in him to see the man's seed crumble. He dispatched her to Lawnview only because the call came in as a suicide. All the detective had to do was stamp the file as such, which would have added a new victory to her clearance rate, but she didn't catch on. Instead, Christy was now before him, tears swelling in her eyes, talking about some estranged serial killer at large. He was indeed for protecting the public but also wanted to help save her career.

"Detective," Sgt. Neal took off his reading glasses, "what is it you're asking of me?"

A bead of sweat rolled down her forehead. "I want some time to work this Natosha Little case."

Not understanding Christy's logic, he asked, "Why so much emphasis on Natosha Little?"

She made no mention of the Bible. "I just think I can crack the offender and these suicides from that angle."

Observing the fire in her eyes, he fell mute for a moment. It wasn't the detective he was worried about. Unbeknownst to her, it was Capt. Dagger who gave him seventy-two hours, beginning at the scene of Natosha, to submit her transfer if she didn't make the cut. He secretly knew the time she was requesting to investigate would be a case of do or die. But if this was how she wanted to go out, that was on her. He did his part.

Sgt. Neal gave Christy a look he was sure she'd never forget. "I hear your request, but I want you to know what this means."

Just by the gaze she figured this was her last shot to tie the game. Determined to follow her own wit, she wouldn't accept failure. "Yes, I know where you're going."

He picked his chin as always when feeling someone was headed towards destruction. "I hope you're not making a mistake."

"Mistakes are experiences. Once we learn from them," she buttoned her jacket, "it becomes a life lesson, and this is mine to learn."

"Okay, if you don't nail this case, say good-bye to your cubical. This department will no longer be your assignment. You got forty-eight hours."

"Thank you." Accepting the ultimatum, she got up and rushed to exit his office.

"Hey, Gatewood," Sgt. Neal yelled out before she could twist the knob, "remember what I told you about chess?"

She inhaled as pride enslaved her tears. "Yes, I do."

He lounged, putting his glasses back on. "The next move is on you, check."

Once inside her car, Christy cried thinking about her father and how the department was so willing to throw her away. She yearned for something at that moment to stop the tears.

BOOK TEN

Officer Bowles was at it again, on duty, far out of his jurisdiction. His eyes were glued to a 2002 Dodge Caravan, Delaware tags. He followed the vehicle up Edmonson Avenue and decided to make a move once it turned onto a deserted block off of Cooks Lane. When his emergency lights were activated, the female motorist pulled over without hesitation.

It wasn't the out-of-state tags that compelled him to make a traffic stop; moreover, the mouth-watering beauty of the driver provided enough probable cause to perform an illegal shakedown. He not only had an affinity for attractive women; weak minded females also never went undetected. All it took was one glance, a certain gesture of the face, an irregular flutter of the eyes, seductive body language, or revealing garments. Those were key signs of low self-esteem, and that's what he preyed on. Rookie or not, the game was understood well.

He first spotted the woman on Hilton Parkway. The way her fingers gripped the thick steering wheel made him squeeze at the crotch of his uniform. She was instantly on his radar. Now a quiet street put her at his mercy. As a standard routine, he switched the name tag. Though the sun just finished its shift, Officer Bowles slid on shades before exiting the car. An aggressive strut advertised his authority. Out came the cruel flashlight.

She rolled down her window, nervously asking, "Is there a problem?"

He tried to blind her. "You ran a light about four blocks back."

She used a palm to deflect the bright assault on her eyes. "I'm sorry, but that wasn't me. I didn't run any lights."

She was attractive up close but looked much better from a distance. A ton of makeup hid physical flaws. Even with a red dress riding up a gorgeous set of thighs, her body was nothing compared to Linda's; nonetheless, it would do. "Are you calling me a liar, ma'am?"

Her natural raspy voice softened, "I'm not calling you anything. People make mistakes. This is a prime example."

Officer Bowles cleverly browsed the empty street. Everything was clear. The van would be used as a shield for what he had in mind. His command was ushered through a stern whisper, "Step out of the car, ma'am."

"Sir, I did nothing wrong."

He shouted loud enough to frighten her. "I'll be the judge of that! Now step the hell out of the vehicle! Won't ask again."

She immediately opened the door. When her heels touched the asphalt, Officer Bowles took a step back to survey her plump backside. If only she granted him permission to play with her pussy, he'd be finish in a snap. Officer Bowles couldn't outright ask her to adhere to an unlawful request, so he welcomed deception as a method of persuasion.

"Do you have any contraband I need to know about?"

Her response was no.

"Well, how about in your van?"

"There's nothing on me or in my car."

He stared at her for a brief second. "I don't think you're being honest."

"Why would I lie?"

"You ask yourself that." A wry smile formed behind his frown. "Turn around and spread your legs."

"Beg your pardon," she looked him up and down, "but I'm wearing a dress."

A gust of lust rained down his spine. He turned off the flashlight, grabbed her arm, and smashed her face against the hood of the van. Now with the woman bent over, he twisted her arm until it cramped. Pain overrode reason, making her afraid, embarrassed, and confused. Officer Bowles hiked up her dress, exposing silk panties. He couldn't see her face but could hear weeping. Being in power turned him on. "I'm only searching you, relax," he uttered to calm her down. If you're clean-"

"I told you already-"

"Let me fucken speak!"

Exhibiting all the precursors of being up to no good, her brain went limp not knowing what to expect.

"If I don't find anything stashed inside your underwear, you are free to go. But if you hinder my search, I'm taking you straight to the big house. Do you understand?"

"Yes."

She complied though truly not in acceptance of what was about to go down. Apparently he was a crazy cop, the type to plant something illegal and haul her off to jail, which was a place she'd never been. In fact, if given a choice, she chose prison over shame. Anything would be better than standing on some side street, dress up, about to get searched by a perverted, psycho officer. She knew this but was too timid to represent her own concerns.

Keeping an arm hemmed behind her back, Officer Bowles ran his free hand over her body. He rubbed her cup-sized breast. The more she shook, the harder his penis got. He would have attempted to sex her had a condom been on hand. It was pure recklessness and stupidity to have his DNA extracted from her womb. But out of the many surfaces the techs could dust for latent prints, vagina wasn't one. So instead of sexually assaulting her, he settled for the cavity search. His fingers couldn't wait to explore the guts of a complete stranger. Officer Bowles caressed her hips; the feel of raw flesh made him grind against her buttocks.

In the process of poking a finger inside of her silk panties, his cell phone rung. The sudden noise yanked the woman out of mild shock. While keeping his subject pinned against the vehicle, he recovered the phone and glanced at the unfamiliar number flashing across the screen. The call was unusual due to not many having his math. For the few who did, Officer Bowles knew those numbers by heart.

The caller hung up, shifting his mood.

"You're breaking my arm," she yelped.

In awe concerning the strange buzz, he almost forgot

about having her limb at a disadvantage. Officer Bowles backed off, allowing her to adjust the dress and turn towards him. She stared at his tag, and he loved this part when a victim thought they could play the snagaroo by remembering his name. Switching up completely, the officer spoke with an inflated chest, "You are a great citizen. I apologize for the inconvenience. Watch those lights from now on. Enjoy the rest of your night. We're done here."

Visibly shook, but glad their encounter didn't go as far as anticipated, she got back behind the comfort of her steering wheel. Despite being violated, she just was happy to drive away.

Inside the cramped space of the patrol car, Officer Bowles located the missed call. As he attempted to redial, the phone rung in his hand. It was the exact same number. Determined as he was cautious, Officer Bowles answered on the third ring, "Yehlow."

A female spoke gently, "Is this a bad time?"

The voice didn't ring a bell.

She picked up on it. "This is Christy Gatewood."

"Oh, hey!" he anxiously chimed. Her correspondence was unexpected. "Bout time you called."

"You busy?"

"Naw, just out playing superman."

"And me," she chuckled, "superwoman. I know the feeling."

"Hurts me none. No big deal. I was taught a good officer is always on duty."

That was an impressive statement. Those were her father's words. "You sound like we had the same teacher."

He kept it simple, "Or just share some of the same ideals. Erase the guesswork."

His conversation really sparked her interest. "I like the way you think. Is that coffee date still on the table?"

Truth was the detective just got in the way of a sweet thing. He had a helpless woman on a lonely street and Christy's call destroyed what could have been an intimate experience. Anger was savored by the taste buds of his soul. "That depends on where you are right now."

"If I told you," she played cat and mouse, "I'd have to kill you."

"Wow, so harsh. At least that murder would take nothing for you to solve."

His humor was appreciated. Surprisingly, with all that tormented Christy's mind, her cheeks still worked. The guy was giving her what she needed. The energy between them created a natural tide for mutual surfing. She rode the wave. "Bowles-"

He flipped the egg over easy. "Call me Tony."

"Okay, Tonnny," she drug the last syllable as his name danced off the tongue, "I'm over east at the moment. Since you're on duty, you probably ain't far from me."

Careful not to stutter, he said, "I was actually making a fast run before you called."

"My bad for barging in."

"No," he corrected her by not making it a big deal, "you're fine. This would be a wonderful time to hook up. Ditch the coffee. Let's grab a bite to eat."

"That would be amazing," she concurred.

While Christy presumably pondered crab dip, he was only thinking about a quick fuck, but it would take work to crack that safe. He first had to make her believe his correspondence posed zero risk. Once he could get her guards down, all else came with the territory. "Where did you have in mind?"

"How about Vision's Bar & Grille in Lutherville?" That was literally her favorite food spot. It was a late hour restaurant that served delicious food at a reasonable price.

"Yeah, I'm down with that joint." Officer Bowles knew exactly where it was but never been inside. With his emergency lights still on, he committed to being there in thirty minutes, give or take.

She accepted the date. "That's perfect for me."

"Sure thing. See you there."

No more needed to be said. Both hung up en route to each other.

* * * *

Something caused Officer Bowles to be late for their rendezvous. Her date hadn't even called to disclose his whereabouts. She rebuked being looked upon as a stalker. Christy bothered not to dial his number; however, time was still of the essence in terms of saving her career. While waiting inside the parking lot of the restaurant, she opened Natosha's dairy.

BOOK ELEVEN

Tod's pupils dilated then adjusted to his favorite part of The Lost Boys. It was the clip where Michael retreated to the lair of a vampire cave to confront his new peers concerning a mysterious wine he was provoked to drink. After taking a sip, his body underwent physical and biological changes, sending him in search of answers. Tod and his wife, Brenda, loved the movie. The VHS cassette played day and night. At seventy-four-years of existence, after being married for nearly three decades, just as Michael in The Lost Boys, Tod had undergone physical challenges. He suffered from almost every ailment a human being could be plagued with.

The elderly man already had one stroke, two heart attacks, high blood pressure, parkinsons disease, and beat prostate cancer. Diabetes stole an eye, and the stroke left half of his face paralyzed; nevertheless, Tod was still a fighter. Even in the face of trials he remained faithful to his deity. It was God who helped him conquer cancer and blessed him with a lifetime partner. Brenda was a supportive spouse, a true example of what it meant to cleave to your mate through sickness and health.

Tod's eye conspicuously escaped the movie and canvassed the bedroom in search of Brenda. He remembered her in a chair beside his bed, but she vanished during his short nap. Oddly, a spiritual emptiness paraded throughout his mind and body. It was a longing, a persistent craving that began as a flicker and quickly transformed into wildfire. Though his wife was accustomed to leaving his presence to prep medications and complete unfinished household chores, something felt different this time.

"Bren!" he shouted, voice blending in with the aggressive volume of the television. He yelled for his wife over and over. Eventually choking on his own phlegm, Tod aimed for a better result by forcing himself to go look for her. She was probably in the basement with that loud washing machine running its course, and the basement was a place in the house he hadn't seen since winter.

Tod elevated the upper body by using the remote to his medical bed. When his frame erected to sitting position, he spasmodically jettisoned one leg off the side of the bed. The task came with difficulty and discomfort. Another thrust dismounted the second leg, causing his foot to violently plunge into the floor. A painstaking ache pervaded throughout his weak bones. Using an aluminum cane along with his feeble arms, Tod managed to free himself from the folds of a soft tomb.

Without the assistance of his wife, a few steps were equivalent to a hundred yard dash, but he fought his way to the bedroom door. Struggling through the hallway, Tod was puzzled as to why every light was on. It was weird being that they were continuously careful to not waste household energy. The hallway linked two unused bedrooms. Both doors were open, televisions and radios were also on blast.

"Bren!" He started to panic. None of what he heard or saw made sense. Mumbling a prayer, he found himself clicking switches, cutting off appliances as he slowly reached the stairwell. From the top step he noticed a flood on the bottom landing. More alarmed than afraid, Tod braved the familiar flight until standing in a swamp up to the ankles. The water was hot enough to sting the skin without creating blisters. A smooth undercurrent manifested a stream between the toes, proving more water flowed from an unknown origin. Two inches higher and live sockets would have transformed the downstairs into an electric chair. He had to prevent further disaster.

The flood got deeper heading to the kitchen. When he got there, the sight of what Tod encountered was too graphic to retain. He was so overwhelmed, heart pounding out of control, that the staff departed from his grip. The distraught husband stood there speechless.

BOOK TWELVE

"Ms. Pretty," he brushed his friend away, "I want to apologize for what happened yesterday. I didn't tell him to do that. Dummy does it to every girl he sees... calls himself trying to put me on the spot. He gets a kick out of it. Forgive me."

Couldn't believe I ran into those same two boys da very next day. We were back in 7Eleven. Unless I was bein' trolled, what a coincidence. Da other dude was da one ta block my path dis time. Dis guy was shorter than his friend. Looked good, smelled great. So what he was put dagether in a well-dressed package, he was still a dirty boy like da rest of dem. Knew he would only play games da same as Lester. Wasn't fa dat. So I looked him in his soft brown eyes and said, "Not interested. You already apologized, now step off."

He flashed white teeth. "Don't be so mean."

Tried my invisible-man-thing again, but the boy's handsome features were too hard ta erase. Wit total concentration, managed ta make half of him disappear, but da rest of him followed me ta da counter. He towered behind me in da small line. When it was my turn, Mrs. Kim greeted me as always, requestin' a scripture fa da day. She did dat every time. Dat was our personal little thang. I thought of somedin fast as she rung up my hot dog. "Fa what does one profit ta gain da world but lose his own soul."

"Good one. Keep up beautiful work," she said.

If only dat Chinese lady knew the type of vicious goodies stashed in my bookbag, she probably wouldn't be commendin' me on scripture. She'd been callin' da police. I kept my cool.

"Dat come to-" she tried da say.

Da voice behind me cut her off, "I'm paying for her food," he put on dat same gorgeous smile, neva once lookin' down at my shoes.

Out of all da drama I heard, boys neva do things fa free. Dey always seek somedin in return. Dat trap was fa da birds, so I looked at him and da cashier in one glance. "No thank you. I got it."

"Nah," he insisted, pullin' out a knot of singles, "keep ya money."

When he handed Mrs. Kim two bucks, dat was da first time a boy been nice ta me. I didn't know whether ta thank him or run out da store.

"Ooookay, Toaha. Got boyfriend. Very nice," she teased while takin' da money.

I was trapped in da middle of a cross fire. My eyes fell ta da buffed tile, catchin' a smeared reflection of myself off da shinny wax. I corrected her, "He's not my boyfriend. Thirteen is a bit young ta be into those things."

Mrs. Kim acted like she didn't hear me. "Today nice boy buy you hot dog, tomorrow he pay rent," she sneered, passin' me a chocolate heart from behind da counter.

As my fingers gripped her gift, thinked about how Lester tricked me wit dat sugar move. Dis boy was tryin' da same ruse, but dis time wit cash. Money came from paper, paper from wood, wood from trees. It was a tree dat God commanded Adam and Eve not ta eat from. Dey were deceived by da Devil, and now dis boy, maybe another imp, was workin' his moves. I went fa it once but neva again. I gave dem both my back ta excuse.

"Wait, sweetheart," he followed me, "what's wrong?"

I told him once outside of 7Eleven, "You don't have ta be so friendly. I can pay fa my own stuff. Besides, don't know you."

"You act like a person never been nice to you."

"Dey haven't." I got close like I was 'bout ta hit him.

"What's your motive, anywhoz?"

He snuffled, "The name's Troy. Maybe you haven't noticed, but we attend the same school. You and the gym teacher, Ms. Denise, be praying together. Am I right?"

Although he was correct, I didn't say a word, just stood there as he continued his rap.

"You stay to yourself and be reading the Bible. I dig that. Was thinking you and I can be friends."

His eyes where deep and wide, da kind made ta pierce da soul. We stared at one another, losin' ourselves. His world suddenly came into color. My reflection in his eyes was much clearer than da waxed floor inside of 7Eleven. From his angle I appeared polished, beautiful, queenly. I almost cheesed. "I'm sorry, Troy. You might be a cool person, but I don't do boys."

"How about girls?"

"Those either." It would have been ova fa any other dude, but he kept on.

"You do God, right?" Troy confirmed.

"Somedin like dat." Now he was talkin' a language I didn't mind listenin' to.

"Before you walk out of my life," he turned his eyes ta dat of a puppy dog, "would you mind holding my hand and saying a prayer?"

He was thinkin' fast on his toes. A boy neva asked me dat. Would of been like sayin' no ta God had I rejected. "Are you givin' me an ultimatum? I consider dem threats."

"Nah, it's your choice. You can either walk away," he held his hands open as if receivin' a present, "or we can share a moment in God together."

I'm not gonna lie, he was makin' my undies wet. Whateva Troy was doin' ta me, da boy was good at it. I put down my hot dog and bookbag, placin' my hands in his. Recalled what happened da last time my eyes were closed, so I kept dem open.

He bowed his head and said, "We pray for those who need a hug and for those who could use some love. Kids who cry themselves to sleep because they have nothing to eat. We pray for the poor bunch, those who come to school just for lunch. Kids who wash their hands before they eat... in a world of confusion, we pray for peace. We pray for children who don't have shoes or clothes, and I personally seek forgiveness while holding the hands of a gentle rose. Amen."

Tory opened his eyes ta me 'bout ta eat him alive. He tapped into apart of me I neva knew existed. Fa some reason dat was da part I wanted ta share wit him. My poor hot dog, put it like dis, I was ready ta stick it in a place other than my mouth. I felt safe and turned on.

"Straight?" he asked, still holdin' my hands.

"..."

"You good?" he asked again.

Dat's when I snapped outta it. "I'm fine."

"You sure?"

"Yes."

"I already gave you my name. What's yours."

I answered his question, and he released my hands. Dat mornin' we walked da school dagether. Almost every mornin' after dat, we met at 7Eleven fa hot dogs. He even sat wit me in da cafeteria. We'd eat buttercrunch and drown chocolate milk. Him two grades above mine brought on unwanted attention from da teachers. It was obvious I had a crush on Troy. I'd scribble his name next ta mine in all my textbooks. Let's not mention da daydreams. In dem he was a knight. I'd be kidnapped by da Devil, held within da depths of hell fire. My knight would show up cloaked in an armor of glory, flexin' on a horse name Death, wieldin' a sword, screamin' hallelujah. He saved me every time.

In school, Troy was respected by all da guys, but there was

always some random girl droolin' ova him. Good thing he didn't take a likin' ta harlots. Dat's why he was so crazy 'bout me 'cause I was reserved. I was his livin' angel, other girls were tunnel rats. Me and Troy's friendship was governed by scripture, so what we began ta feel fa each other was acceptable by God. Our chemistry was divine.

A marked car pulled into the parking lot of the restaurant, and Christy closed the book in time to watch it navigate alongside the Grand Marquise. Officer Bowles got out of his vehicle with flashlight in hand. He slid over to the driver side and lightly tapped the tinted window.

Assuming the detective would be angry at his lateness, he used a brief stage play to break the ice. "Excuse me, Ms. Lady, but I'm going to need you to step out of the car."

Christy was on stuck but found humor in playing along. She rolled down the window. "Something the matter?"

"Yes, there is." He practiced his lines on the detective, secretly wishing she was one of his victims. "I reckon you are aware of slaying two lights a mile back."

Following suit, she tamed a smile. "Sorry, wasn't paying attention."

"No one ever is." He opened her car door. "Feet on the gravel."

Christy got out of the whip, slammed the door, and stood within arm's reach of her compadre. "Would you really like to know the reason why I ran those lights?"

He seen a controlled flame in her eyes. "Thrill me."

"Ran those lights because I was trying to be on time for a dinner date. You see," she folded her arms, "he never showed up, and now I'm here all alone."

"Hmmmm, sad story. I'm certain your date had a legitimate excuse, but impatience is no reason to break the law." Officer Bowles took out his cuffs. "I can take you to jail... or-"

"Or what, officer?" she pouted.

If only the detective knew how much she was feeding into his sickness. "Or you can forget about your date and let me replace him. I'll be sure to make up for his shortcomings."

They both smiled, bringing their dramatic performance to a halt. She now got on serious time, jabbing at his vest. "You hit those lines on every lady you pull over?"

"Nah," he weaseled his way out, "those were just for you."

"I bet." She smirked. "Let's head in."

"Ladies first," he responded, happy to have a personal foul resolved so easily.

* * * *

The air was light with the aroma of hot pastries. A white female greeted them at the door, "Welcome to Vision's Bar & Grille. Got a reservation or are you guys dropping in?"

"The second one." Christy smiled at the petite woman. "Do you have any tables available?"

The simper was returned. "Yes, we have a lovely table for two in the non-smoking section. Will that do?"

"Perfect," stated Officer Bowles, "we'll take what we can. Beggars can't be choosy."

She escorted them through an array of tables on the floor. Each were occupied. The pair were seated in the rear of the restaurant in a cream, heart-shaped booth. The cream was the same shade as Linda Foreman's home. A candle burned at the center of the table. Classic Rock played from the jukebox. It set the emotional tone, especially for older couples. Christy was impressed by the level of peace. The place always played good music.

To the contrary, Officer Bowles preferred hip-hop. All other genres were considered a waste of musical instruments, but it wasn't about him at that moment. It was about Christy, making her feel like she was at the center of the universe, when she was really the farthest planet from his sun. For a moment, an alter ego depicted the detective as not just another piece of ass. Her dominate traits gravitated him. She was outspoken and strong willed, the sort of girl he wouldn't normally prey on, but he accepted the challenge.

"Wow," Officer Bowles spat, "this is nice."

"Yes, it is," muttered Christy, reaching for the menu. Hitting the wee hours, the scent of eggs was a dead giveaway of the chef preparing for a morning rush.

A perky waitress pranced over. She waved and bowed in one swift motion. "Hey, I'm Tina, and I will be taking your order. Do y'all have an idea of what you'd like to eat?"

Tina's features were innocent, owning a face so pretty it appeared three-dimensional. She had a modeling frame, orange streaks peeking through long locks. Officer Bowles got instantly aroused while studying the exotic teenager. He glanced back and forth at her and Christy, comparing strengths and weaknesses. Both were hard to choose from.

"Yup," Christy closed the menu, "I'll have the peach hotcakes, sausage, eggs, and milk.

He ordered the same thing, hoping that would please Christy by showing interest in what she liked. When the waitress glided away, the detective asked questions about what influenced him to become a cop. Abreast with her father's history, Officer Bowles decided to use the obvious as ammunition when launching his ploy. "I was born in Upstate New York. I'm the only child. My mom was the pastor of a hole-in-the-wall church-"

She never heard of a place of God labeled as such. "Why call it that?"

"Because it was more of a soup kitchen than a place of spiritual liberation. It was a church for homeless people who reduced God to a cup of coffee and a tuna sandwich."

"For the sake of argument... I'll leave that alone," she uttered, raising a brow.

"My mother was a good woman, bought me up as close to scripture as possible. Meanwhile, dad was a cop who never climbed in rank. He gave the department his all but gained nothing."

A chill froze Christy. "Amen. That's relatable."

"And after years of blood, sweat, and service, my dad was murdered trying to stop a robbery in progress."

"That is so bad," the chill fizzled into numbness, "you can't be serious."

"Sure is," he murmured, gaining the response intended.

"My dad was murdered also," she compassionately shared. "Have you heard of Raymond Gatewood?"

He scratched his head to display an expression of contemplation. "Don't think so."

Her voice cracked, "He was a homicide lieutenant who got murdered at a gas station ten years back..."

Officer Bowles shook his head. "Can't recall ever hearing about that name or situation."

The oxygen in her lungs expelled through one nostrils. It was almost impossible to be a member of the force and not hear rumors about her father nor his reputation. Instructors even used his name as a reference in the academy. All the same, maybe Raymond's buzz spared Tony or simply hadn't reached him yet. She gave her date a way out, "I mean, the incident did happen ten years ago. The world has drastically changed since then. Foolish of me to think my father would be a topic in every household; he wasn't Martin Luther King or anything."

"But I'm sure your dad played his part to the fullest."

"Tony, you don't have to," she repelled, "let's just change that topic."

Her energy was off, eyes too heavy to play the bubbly role. He seen through her cloud of pain. He figured she probably needed a hug, ear, or shoulder to lean on. "If there is something troubling you, if I spoke out of turn-"

The detective's lips slightly shuddered as if she wanted to say something but didn't know where to start. "You said nothing wrong."

"Then," the chase was on, "what is it? You can talk to me. That's what friends are for."

His statement was self-explanatory. As if she didn't know who to trust, her demeanor was one of doubt. "My mind is everywhere, I guess."

"We can work out whatever it is, together. Let's share your burden. Give it a shot." His hands found hers.

Christy admired his willingness to provide comfort without stipulations, but Natosha's case was too ripe to discuss. Frankly, it would probably sound stupid that she put her career on the line trying to connect two suicides, both tied together by mere coincidence. Better yet, blaming a mystery serial killer as the perpetrator. And, finally, betting her chips on a diary that, so far, was no more than a teenage love story.

Still and all, Bowles was the first uniform to report to the scene of Natosha Little. Not just that, he also led her to a key that unlocked more than a front door. If anyone was capable of understanding her plight, perhaps he was that person, so she decided to use his friendly insight to weigh the evidence gathered so far. Thinking about how to put her dilemma into words, she unintentionally glanced at his name tag. The discrepancy encouraged curiosity. So, instead of discussing what really had her perplex, she presented a question that caught him in a headlight.

"Tony," she uttered, "are you aware that your name tag says Owings?"

Letting her hands go, he fumbled with the front of his uniform, taking a double and triple look at the tag. It said Owings clear as day. Officer Bowles tried to play it off. "Now... how did that happen. I must of picked up the wrong shirt in the locker room."

Christy ingested it as a simple mistake. "Made a little boo-boo, huh?"

To him negligence of any kind was a strike against

self, a way to get him jammed up. In truth, he forgot to switch the tag after his last traffic stop. The interruption of the detective's phone call took him off of his game. Officer Bowles resisted reaching back across the table. He threw a fit, "It's crap like this that piss me off."

She couldn't understand the sudden switch of attitude. "Why are you flipping out over an honest mishap? It happened. Get over it. Move on."

"You're right." He started sweating. Feeling their outing was destroyed, the nervous man still attempted to rebound their initial conversation. "Now... where were we? What was you saying-"

He got interrupted by the waitress, "Here you go," she uttered, placing one plate at a time on the table. "Sorry it took so long."

"That's okay," responded Christy, eye-fucking the food.

"The cooks don't usually fall asleep with a pot on the stove. Enjoy. Be back if you need something else," the waitress promised then sped off.

Officer Bowles lifted his cheek with a phony grin. "This looks delicious."

"Doesn't it," she concurred, clutching a fork.

Not once reaching for utensils, he goggled at his watch. "Oh, shit. Excuse my language."

"What?" she was addled.

He stood. "I got to skip."

"Why? We just got here. Finish your food first."

"I can't. Didn't realize it was so late. I got some important paperwork to do before I punch out. I'm totally sorry."

Christy didn't know what to say when he removed a fifty dollar bill from his wallet and placed it down on the table. She pushed it away.

"Nah, that's the least I can do for running out on you," he pledged. "I would really like to finish this off. Can I call you later?"

"Guess so." Her spirits took a plunge. She didn't accredit his mental shift to the discovery of a bogus name tag. This situation reminded her so much of what was last read. Christy empathized with Natosha's take, men came with too many extra features. The woman was grateful to still be a virgin.

"Make it up to you," he promised.

She gave that frivolous wave of the hand. "Don't worry

about it. I'm good."

He dismissed himself without prejudice.

Before Christy knew it, she was at the table alone. With steam coming from the pancakes, she couldn't see them go to waste. The detective took the diary from her purse and rested it beside her plate. She planned to read while devouring her meal.

BOOK THIRTEEN

Me and Troy dated throughout middle school. We kept us a secret 'cause we were nobody's business. When more speculations arose, me and my love gave each other space. Shoo, I'd even let him flirt wit other girls ta throw people off, but we knew what da real was. Eventually, da whole school knew we were an item. In eighth grade, my gym teacher, Ms. Denise, kept me after recreation ta have a chat.

"Please, Natosha, have a seat," she said with her palms dagether in a humble manner.

As I took ta da bleaches, a thousand things ran through my mind, but my face didn't show it. Ms. Denise was one of da cool instructors. First she taught seventh grade before decidin' ta bump up her game by takin' ova da gym schedule. She was shaped like a pear but had more energy than most of her students.

Ms. Denise sat beside me. "You know why I kept you behind, right?"

"Um-ummmm," I answered, shakin' my head no.

She gave me the wryneck, flashin' those motherly eyes.

"It's about that boy, Troy. I was young once... long, long time ago," a sparkle glittered within her pupils, "so I know how it feels to have a crush on someone. But what we do with our desires makes them good or bad, not just having the desire itself."

I purposely kept a dumbfounded expression as if I didn't have a clue.

She read my face and said, "You can act like you don't know what I'm saying, but, Natosha, I'm sure you do. Look, your grades are up, and I don't want you throwing that away over some rinky-dink boy. That young man is trouble. You may not see it, but I do."

Hearin' her badger Troy, I wiggled my foot ta let off steam. Had ta defend our secret, "Ms. Denise, me and Troy are only friends-"

"Yes, darling, I'm sure."

"But I'm-"

"What you are experiencing is puppy love. That's it."

Why was she actin' like some psychologist, desperately tryin' ta hypnotize me? Da lady wouldn't let me speak.

"Does your mother know about this relationship you have?" she deceptively asked.

I glanced at da basketball court, den da doors of da

gymnasium, den back at da bleaches, anything ta avoid lookin' directly at her. My jittery behavior must of answered her question.

"Stay in the good book. Leave that boy alone. Do you understand me, young lady?" she asked.

Her request resembled a command. I stood and agreed just ta get her off my back, "Yes, ma'am."

"You can go now, but not without some fire under your butt to keep you on point."

Whateva dat meant. Her words got lighter as I moved farther away, until da sound of her voice completely disappeared. I assumed she was still babblin' after I exited da gym.

Instead of meetin' Troy after school, I walked straight home. Everythin' was peaceful until I got ta da house. Mommy must heard me turn da key 'cause she was shoutin' before I got inside.

"Tosha! Get dat little hot ass in here."

I dashed ta da back of da house ta find Mommy settin' at da edge of her bed. In one hand she had Mr. Paul's belt, da house phone was in da other. I let da book bag slide down my back onto da floor.

"Bitch," she muttered wit both eyes squinted, "you got school teachers callin' my damn house talkin' 'bout how hot chu is!"

As I tried ta explain, Mommy hurled da phone at me but missed. Good thing her aim was off or my head would of been leakin'. Usin' da belt as her weapon of choice, she rushed ova and began beatin' me like a runaway slave. I blocked, ducked, weaved, and dodged all while standin' in place.

"I done tol' chu [SHHWAAK!] not ta [SHAAWEK!] make me look bad. If dem people take you off my check [SHHWAK! SWWEEK! SWWIK!] I'm gone half-kill you in nis house!"

I cried in pain, still feelin' da sting of dat thick, leather belt. My soft skin was coverd in welts. As I fought ta catch my breath, she circled me like a drill sergeant.

"Da next time I hear 'bout dat thug or any other boy of dat matter," she grabbed me by da hair, "you'll wish I didn't. Now get outta my face!"

Like a human rag doll, she slung me into da hallway and slammed da door so hard da knob flew off. I could hear her still fussin', bitch dis, bitch dat. Da pitch of my sobbin' was reduced ta a silent burble. I escaped into da nursery of my room. Mommy continued ta rant as I studied my wounds. Da welts were already turnin' red.

As those wounds transformed before my eyes, I was subdued by a strange rage. Stranded someplace between joy and pain, the enigma made me chuckle ta myself. Wit tears runnin' down my face, dat chuckle turned into a devilish smirk. I used my tongue, like an injured animal, and slowly licked da wounds on my arms. I ran a hand all ova my body, caressin' every part. Wondered why Ms. Denise told Mommy 'bout a matter she couldn't prove. Seen bad things happenin' ta her. Maybe a heart attack or butchery... death by electrocution or suffocation, drownin' or poisonin'. Whateva da cause, it had ta be painful and unexpected. Since I was in no shape ta kill my gym teacher, thought 'bout givin' Troy my V-card just ta get even wit Mommy, but would dat be enough ta soothe my anger? A small box cutter on da dresser caught my eye; dat, too, belonged ta Mr. Paul, loaned ta me fa a school project. It's glint gave me a supernatural feelin'. When I picked it up, a power source charged me wit more evil thoughts. I was tempted ta use da box cutter on Mommy, but how could I imagine such a sin. Da Bible taught me ta honor my parents so dat my days would be long upon da earth. It was then dat an angle spoke ta me, tellin' me ta put down da box cutter. My stomach felt upset. Dizziness made da room spin. My head was featherweight.

Da angel whispered again, "If your hands cause you to sin, cut them off."

In my line of view were two heat pipes, six inches apart, stretchin' vertical from floor ta ceilin'.

Da angel then said, "For it is better to enter the Kingdom of God with one hand than to go to hell with both hands."

I drifted ova ta da steel pipes, placed my slender arm between them and yanked. Da more I thinked 'bout hurtin' Mommy, I got angrier and yanked harder, applyin' more pressure until my bone snapped.

"AHHHHHH!" I screamed as my arm dangled, blackin' out.

"How was the meal?" a voice said, interrupting Christy's concentration.

Placing a finger on the last word read, her eyes drifted to the waitress. "It was tasty."

The waitress played with her fingers. "Can I get you something else?"

Christy smirked. "No, in fact, I was just about finished."

"I'm not rushing you-"

"Of course you're not, but fetch me the check when you get a chance, please. Thank you."

The waitress made an amicable head gesture and sprung off.

The detective put the book away. She was fixated on the life of the victim. Whereupon, Natosha appeared to be everything but a true believer of God. Stuck in an illusion, she was far from an angel, more closer to a sociopath if anything. Natosha allowed her anger to transform into homicidal thoughts; hence, in an effort to mute those destructive ideas, the child had to literally break an arm to prevent harming her own mother. If Natosha maintained thoughts about hurting others, there was a great chance she probably did commit suicide. The mention of a box cutter, especially when Linda Foreman was found gripping one in her hand, seemed like a weird set of circumstances.

At that point Christy felt digging into Natosha's case

was the worst career move she could have made. Reiterating facts in her mind once more, Natosha had a fight with her mom, just as she did in her diary, but, instead of breaking an arm, this time she ended her own life. Christy began to become more interested in why Natosha killed herself, rather than being murdered. The truth was clear cut. Obverse to an option to work the file, she had to save her job, and what better way of doing so then to call Neal and own up to her miscalculation, which would be her last chance to close both cases as suicides. That would buy her more time to work on some other fresh murder case. Hope wasn't lost; everything was still up for grabs. She just had to make the call.

The waitress returned with the check. Christy paid the bill and blessed the teenager with a handsome tip. Getting up from the table, the detective checked her cell phone. No signal. With a full belly and the jukebox still bumping good music, Christy hurried to the exit in a forward motion.

BOOK FOURTEEN

Christy got an excellent phone signal inside the car. Three missed calls and two messages demanded her urgent attention. One number was blocked, the other two were from headquarters. She checked the two messages without delay. When the first one came on, nothing. After ten seconds of listening to the silent message, Christy heard heavy breathing in the background. It was difficult to tell if the sound came from a male or female, but someone was definitely playing on her phone. The message was erased. "Next!" she blurted, moving right along to the last one.

"Detective Gatewood," Sgt. Neal assertively uttered into the receiver, "I've been trying to reach you. Your darn phone keeps jumping to the answering machine. When you get this message, give me a ring back. And make it snappy."

Being so anxious to return his call, Christy immediately hung up. As the number was dialed, she practiced her spiel aloud, "Hey, Sgt. Neal, you were right. These cases are just suicides, and I would like to be placed back into rotation. Can we forget about that talk at the office? I want to close these cases and start over." Her rehearsal concluded before the call went through.

"Baltimore Homicide Unit," answered Sgt. Neal, his gruff voice never failing as a signature trait.

"Hello, this is Christy. I got your message. I didn't have good service at the time. What's up?"

He chastised her off the jump, "What a prime example of why it's mandatory detectives carry walkie-talkies and be assigned to unmarked vehicles, but, of course, you wouldn't know anything about that."

"I apologize," she mumbled. Christy was in the wrong and planned to dance around that topic as always. However, while in an apologetic mood, now was the best time to apologize for everything else as well. "I ran across some more info concerning Natosha Little and-"

"Save your breath..." he took the floor, "there's been another suicide."

"When? Where? Who?" Christy asked, forgetting about the speech she practiced.

"The call came in an hour ago. The address is a couple of doors down from your initial victim... yes, Natosha Little. The new victim is an elderly woman."

The detective was rendered senseless. Her gut knew it was the neighbor she interviewed. Though her mind was on a seesaw, Christy kept calm to show she had everything under

99

control. "I'm on it."

Sgt. Neal was cavalier, donning an attitude no different from calling a fast-food joint to place an order. "The victim is a Brenda Webb, and the address-"

"No need," she stopped him while starting up the car, "I know where it's at."

He recognized the detective's confidence in her own homework. "I'm not saying it is, but, just maybe, your theory has some logic to it. There is a pattern, and if it's some animal out there killing these women, I want that person in a cage!" the sergeant uttered through gritted teeth.

"I will see to that," she promised, voice expressing a self-assurance that erased all doubt. Never again would she second guess herself.

"Keep me informed," said Sgt. Neal. Those three words ended their conversation.

At full throttle, Christy rushed to the new location.

* * * *

The damp pavement bore witness to a recent flood. Christy examined the mess as she passed a handful of

officers huddled together upon the porch. All voices were
at a whisper as if arranging for their next play. Though
the street was speckled with few emergency vehicles, it
seemed the victim's house was temporarily converted into an
officers' lounge. As the detective entered the home, she
was bumped, almost ran over by a forensic specialist.
"Well, excuuse me," she stated, appalled.

The Hispanic male never turned to apologize, which made
her feel like a ghost or some unwanted spirit. Being
careful not to slip on the wet floor, she sailed through
the congested living room. A slender hallway led her
straight to the kitchen. When entering that part of the
house, just as with Tod, Christy was blown aback. In
addition to the wrinkled, naked body hanging from a light
fixture on the ceiling, the presence of her nemesis struck
the woman with disgust. Chance and Miles stood near the
body. Chance was apparently collecting evidence while his
partner manned a camera.

Detective Miles caught a glimpse of Christy approaching.
"Gatewood," he called out, not at all surprised.

Chance formed a smile at the sound of her name.

Christy reeled back a step before asking, "What are you
two doing here?"

101

Her question offended Miles, causing Chance to arrogantly respond, "Take a moment and ask yourself the same thing."

"This is my damn investigation!" she roared.

"No," Miles tried to shush her by holding up an index finger, "correction... this is ouurrr investigation now."

The kitchen began to spin just as Natosha's room did the day she stuck her arm between those pipes. In a state of distress, almost doubling over, Christy placed a palm to her forehead and leaned against the wall.

"Hold up, Detective," uttered Chance, hoping to add insult to injury, "that wall is part of evidence."

She totally blew him off, saying to herself, "This is so not happening."

"Why isn't it?" asked Miles. "I mean, last time I checked, this is our job description. So just as the early bird catches the worm," he couldn't resist flashing his brown teeth, "she who is slow to respond loses her turn."

Christy resurrected her mental balance with haste. "This is much bigger than what you think."

"I bet it is," Miles uttered, mockingly. "And what it is, hummp, is no bigger than what you see." He stared at the corpse. "What I'm looking at is an old woman named

Brenda Webb. She was discovered by her husband who, by the way, suffered from a heart attack after he phoned the police. God only knows why this woman hung herself with an extension cord, but this was a suicide, nothing more."

Chance assisted his partner, "If you say suicide, suicide it is, pal."

Their opinions were fashioned out of spite, so Christy took it upon herself to point out a noticeable discrepancy. "How did this brittle woman get all the way up there to hang herself?" She pointed to the large gap between the victim's feet and the floor. "I don't see no chair or ladder around."

Chance was fast to say, "Maybe her husband removed whatever she used before he made the call. As you can see," he spun the corpse to the right, "the cord is almost wrapped around her jowl. This proves her husband was probably pulling on her feet to yank her down."

As much as Miles believed Christy wasn't fit for the job, he had to concur that his partner's interpretation of the scene was pretty lame. He could have conjured up a better hypothesis, something more plausible. "Wait..." Miles posed a rhetorical question, speaking in general, "what husband you know pulls on his wife's feet to get her down from hanging?"

Chance attempted to justify his own bogus scenario with a touch of humor, "Some people are backwards like that. At times my nose run, and my feet smell-"

"Use common sense," she interceded, sticking to the matter at hand, "whoever hung Brenda Webb pulled on her feet to make sure she was dead."

Miles paused in thought, taking a remote interest in Christy's theory. He sensed she was hinged to something big and wanted to steal her glow. Fighting with the woman was the wrong approach. To get the facts, Miles figured it wise to use honey instead of vinegar. The detective lowered his voice, "Gatewood, you're withholding something. Come on, tell us what you're working on. If we work together on whatever you're doing, we three can close it faster. What do you say?"

Instead of giving him the finger, she said, "I'm not on to anything. But if I was, why should I trust you two?"

Miles exposed his intensions by that greedy look in his eyes. "Because we're buds, maybe your last hope. Now, if you refuse to spill the beans," he turned off the camera so his threat wouldn't be recorded, "we will find out, and then-"

She stood her ground. "Then what?"

"We'll make shit real bad for you. By the time we're finished, you'll be dancing at one of those strip clubs on Baltimore Street," Miles vowed.

"And you would go through all of that just to prove a point," she said with a shake of the head. "My situation shouldn't be that important as to take you out of your way."

"See, that's the thing," Miles called himself coming clean, "it's not out of my way. You rode that daddy card far too long, had it easy while detective's like me and my partner bust our balls on every case, no help. In this department each hand should carry its own weight, no matter the gender. Your father worked for the department; he didn't create it. You may not want to open your eyes to this, but it's guys like me who keep them jails filled up. Good, hard police work is what substantial reputations are made of. They might not ever forget your father, but, if it's up to me, they'll never remember you."

She wanted to punch the man in the face but chose to be the bigger person. "If it's that much hate in your heart, do what you feel. Don't let me stop you, but I'll win in the end," she stated with conviction.

Chance couldn't wait to leap back into the conversation. He supported his partner by saying to her, "Don't take this personal, but women belong in the kitchen, not arbitrating for the dead."

She bounced back with the first thing that came to mind, "And two fags belong screwing each other and not trying to ruin someone's career."

As Christy turned to leave, Chance shouted out, "Now you're finished! Forty-eight hours... you'll need more than that to save your job."

Other uniforms gave an inquisitive look as she exited the front door. Chance and Miles were trying to extort her, but she refused to bow to them. Regardless of how much she despised both detectives, it didn't subtract an iota from their credentials. They were, nonetheless, professionals. A threat from either man was one to be taken seriously. With them now trying to shake her tree, she had to be careful. Christy understood their gripe against her, and both picked the perfect time to let it surface. But how did they know what buttons to push? How did they know that her career was on a brink of destruction? Only one man could have given them access to her personal business, and she wanted to know why.

BOOK FIFTEEN

"Put your fuckin' hands up!" an officer demanded.

Tony opened his eyes, beaming down the barrel of a shotgun.

"I will blow your head off if you so much as cough! You're under arrest for the murder of Natosha Little, Linda Foreman, and Brenda Webb."

Tony lied helpless on his sofa until those steel bracelets crackled around his wrist.

Suddenly he awoke, jumping up in a cold sweat, uniform drenched. His chest heaved, heart raced, and eyes bounced off the walls before realizing he was home. The man had yet another nightmare. Bad dreams became the norm whenever he closed his lids. Most of his furniture was lightweight, making his one bedroom apartment so empty that he could shout and an echo would whisper back. The man was a nomad, used to packing up to switch locations at a moments notice. Being able to disappear without any attachments tugging him back, that was his preference. Throughout life he settled in different states, and out of everywhere he'd been, Baltimore was his love, the one place that contained most of his memorable experiences. As a bona fide native of New York, not a soul would guess his origin unless he told them. Tony learned to conceal his upstate drawl for personal reasons. How could he expose his true self to the world? If he shared his true story, he feared everyone would define him as a poison. So he kept his situation a secret.

Tony composed himself through meditation, dwelling on he and Christy's last encounter, how something as stupid as a name tag got in the way. It saw Christy as a hooker and wanted to take advantage of the detective by aborting self-confidence, willpower, and her womanhood. It desired to upset the balance of her universe, slaughtering whatever principle that fed her motivation to live. On the reverse, Tony's distant side yearned for a companion. Christy's strong mind and pleasant disposition made her the ideal mate. The stars shined on her end, but for him it was too late. A woman paved the way for his downfall, and he would be at odds with the opposite sex until breaking even.

There was no happiness in his life. Lately he payed less attention to his surroundings, taking more chances than usual, overwhelming himself with worldly desires instead of focusing on the small things. For instance, he hadn't took a decent shower or washed his uniform since obtaining it. He no longer was living for self; It had taken over. In fact, for the past few weeks, he hadn't made it pass the living room of his apartment. He would come in fatigued, collapsing upon his sofa. Truth of the matter was he excluded the back of his home. The bedroom door stayed locked because that's where It had the most influence over him.

The nightmares were ten times as horrible when sleeping in his own bed, and in the bed was where It would pick his brain. He was better off on the sofa, staying safe by keeping It locked away. For whenever the bedroom door was ajar, the killing would start again. But, even as a law enforcement officer, he accepted the murders; furthermore, Tony felt he had no choice. At first the killing would take place every so often, now they were happening almost every night. The gravity of being apprehended weighed on his conscience. Sure, he loved to solicit and violate helpless females, but that was as far as it went. It told him that women were toxic, and those same infested women had to die. That was the Lord's creed.

"Tony... open this door..." a voice came from the bedroom.

He tried to shun it by convincing himself that the voice was a figment of his imagination. It wasn't real, so he wasn't obligated to respond. The rough twist of the door knob stole his attention.

It called out again, "Tony, let us out of this room! It's lonely in here."

Tony placed both hands against his ears to block out the sound. It was being deceptive, trying to get out to sift information as it always does.

After a minute of hearing a pulse beat through his palms, his ears were released. As soon as he liberated his sense of sound, the voice yelled out again.

"What are you thinking?"

Some how It was aware, examining his every movement, or was it that he and It were one.

"You can talk to us. Tell us what's on your mind... let's share it," the voice suggestively uttered.

Under the crack of the door, he could see It's shadow moving from side to side. His bedroom was a straight shot from the sofa.

"I know you can hear us... say something!" It shouted.

"I'm here... I'm here," he responded, slighting his view away from the door.

"We're thinking about her... aren't we?"

"I'm not thinking about anyone or anything," he lied, turning his back to the door.

It paused, then invidiously continued, "We know when you're lying. What would cause you to lie to us, huh?" the voice questioned, but the answer was dismissed with silence. "Tony, this is why we must get rid of her. She's just like the rest of them, evil. We don't need anyone else but us."

"Shuuut up!" he shouted, arms crossed, embracing himself. "I had enough of these murders. They won't come looking for you. In my dreams... they never do. I'm the one who's going to burn for this. They'll put me to death by lethal injection."

"We're born to die," the voice retorted. "Have we forgot who put us in this situation?"

He lobbed both hands over his sweat-drenched face.

"Tony," It persisted, "we must kill her!"

He cried out, "Why? What have she done to us? She isn't like the other helpless ones. She strong-"

"Foolishness!" It objected. "We've murdered other innocent people just like her. In the end, we found out that those people weren't as innocent as they proclaimed.

This is what we're good at; this is what we are called to do."

Tony wept as reality struck him like lightening. It was right. Their divine duty was to sort out the demons of the world and put them to death. Above all else, though It wasn't aware, the detective had already gained knowledge of his alias name tag. It was only a matter of time before she caught on. Tony weighed all the pro's and con's in a single thought, arriving at his senses. "I guess... you're right." He faced the bedroom door. "She must die."

"Yesss!" It cheered. "Do it tonight. Let us out, now."

Tony could hear It jumping up and down on the bed, happily. "There is no need to let you out. I'll do this one alone."

The jumping stopped.

Light footsteps rushed back to the door. "It's not your mission to do it on your own," It iterated. "Together, for we are one and always will be."

"I'll take care of it tonight... tonight if we meet up," Tony assured, lips contorted, anger brewing in his pitch. What It didn't know was that Christy would be his one and only kill, even if he had to leave It behind and start over.

It fell silent, thinking, perhaps unsure. But It could do nothing while locked away besides trust him and await for night to fall. He wouldn't let It down; he never did. "You are doing the world a justice," It uttered before becoming mute. It's shadow faded from beneath the door.

Tony stayed in place, contemplating, picturing the detective dead. That was his ritual, a thing he would always do before the actual event. He had to first kill that person in his mind. The rest was predicated on the perfect time and opportunity. He was an angel of death, yet in human form. It was sent to him to ensure God's will be done. It, too, was an angel of death, yet everything but human... so it seemed.

BOOK SIXTEEN

Detective Gatewood barged into the annex office. Enraged to the tenth power, all professionalism went out the window. Sgt. Neal squinted as she rudely expressed herself, "Bastard, you've betrayed me after earning my trust! How could you?"

His voice was relaxed, "What the hell are you talking about?"

She furiously yelled, "Don't try to pull a wool over my eyes. You dispatched Miles and Chance to the scene of Brenda Webb. I'm the one investigating these suicides."

"I called you first," his baritone deepened, slowly slipping away from a stable composure, "got no answer. In fact, called twice, even left a message on your voice mail. You tell me, was the body of this woman suppose to wait until you got ready to pick up the phone? Time waits for no one."

That wasn't what she was trying to hear. "Why send Chance and Miles opposed to someone else?"

Forced into a position to explain his judgement, as though she was his supervisor, plucked his nerves. "I sent my best men. You fail to realize that I have a job to perform, and this division doesn't revolve around you, Chance, or Miles!"

That's when Christy got nonchalant, shooing him with that discarded hand gesture, "The fuck ever."

It was that body language that made him pissed. Off came the glasses as the tone of his voice elevated, "I want this garbage solved before the big guys put me on the menu. I don't need the FBI involved."

"Oh, that's what this is all about, you?"

He lost control, spittle flew from his lips, "Don't you run me that shit, not after all the times I covered your ass. You would have already been out of this division if it wasn't for me!"

She returned fire, "If it's just about this rare string of suicides being solved, what do the status of my career have to do with that? How did Chance and Miles know details about the conversation we had?"

He defended his position, "I know nothing about that though I did send them to the scene, yes. That's it."

"Oooohh, pleeeese, then how did they know about the forty-eight hours you gave me? Answer that..." she inquired, eyes wide.

He sported a confused expression, face locked in

thought. That certainly was a good question, especially since it wasn't him who shared that information. In essence, the detective was tackling these cases alone, so he sincerely sent the men out to give her a hand, for three heads were mathematically better than one.

The screaming subsided as Christy's emotions got the best of her. She disintegrated into tears. "If you didn't tell them, who did?"

Like a vampire caught in ultraviolet rays, he watched her fall apart before his eyes. Searching for a legitimate answer, an invisible cloud of penitence hovered above his head, yet the matter was too complexed to fish out a simplistic explanation. If the men were familiar with her personal situation, the information came from someone up top. His tone sympathetically regressed, "Can't tell you who told them, but it wasn't me. Perhaps, that answer doesn't satisfy your curiosity, but it's the truth."

"Are you telling me that..." tears continued to race down her face, "there's a leak somewhere in this department, an enemy who wants to get rid of me?"

Her supposition was on point, but he knew better to openly agree. "I won't say that-"

"Then... what... are... you... saying?" she spoke slow

enough for her inquisition to sink in. "If that leak is an enemy of mine, he was most likely an enemy of my dad."

Again, the detective had a right to her own opinion, even if it was incorrect. "Christy, I have no proof of what you're assuming. All I know is I sent Chance and Miles out to assist you."

She refused to go for that. "You sent them out to hurt me."

He wanted to stand but stayed seated. "Watch it. Don't overstep your badge. I am where I'm at today because of your father. It wasn't me who gave you the forty-eight hours; I was only following orders."

She read the sincerity in his gaze. Maybe It wasn't him who wished to get rid of her; it was somebody else, someone with more power and authority. An adversary, camouflaged within the echelon of the department, who wanted to see her suffer. Her clearance rate was just an instrument this person used as a weapon.

"When I look at you," now his eyes got watery in reminiscent of the past, "I see your old man. The guy was always determined just like you. He never spoke about his home life," the sergeant coughed up a smirk, "I mean, we were unsure if he even had one. His character never contradicted the badge. This line of work was second nature to him, his life."

Christy finally gained the strength to cut off the sprinklers.

"But I started to see a change in him, his attitude."

The mention of the word 'change' made her earlobes twitch. She, too, witnessed his strange behavior at home.

Sgt. Neal blabbered on, "Raymond began to work longer hours, just tons of paperwork. I believe he was on the verge of exposing something real big, but whatever that something was went to the grave with him."

Giving eye-to-eye contact, she asked, "Can you tell me the last case he worked?"

"That's the thing, nobody in this division knows. His desk was left empty, so was his locker. Strange... huh?" His intent stare matched hers. "If your dad was losing his mind, and I say this with love and respect, I don't want the same to happen to you. I threw them suicides your way to lend a helping hand, but you used that hand as a shovel to dig your own grave. I'm proud of you, and I believe in you." A lone tear, one within the sergeant's right eye, finally forced its way into freedom. Amazingly, it evaporated just as quick as it fell.

She leaned forward to add emphasis, "If I was a victim, I'm only doing what I hope some other detective would do for me."

He wanted to be sure she totally understood his position, "I appreciate your determination; I'm all for it, but I don't want you to lose it if this blows up in your face."

His concern was heartfelt. "It's not what we go through, it's what we get through. It feels like I already lost everything, but when you hit rock bottom, the only path left is up. I know how it feels to lose a human being you love. These victims are more than just a case or another number added to the board. They were people, flesh and blood. If doing my job means losing my job, then whoever initiated my time limit was right... this division isn't for me. Closing out these cases, doing it just to save a career, would be me allowing these victims to be killed twice. This time... by my hands. Even you said a writer is only as good as his last book, but a book can only be written one word at a time. With these murders, they can only be solved one clue at a time, and I'm trying my hardest to piece this thing together."

He weaved her soft ball. "Speaking of clues," the

sergeant pulled out his desk drawer, brandishing a manila envelope, "here's the lab reports and photos that were taken at the scene of Natosha Little."

Subdued by a sudden trance, her hand slowly retrieved the envelope, praying that it contained the lead she needed to crack the case. Time did stand still.

Before Christy was able to read the results, he broke her spell by saying, "The lab found nothing useful. No finger prints, hair follicles, or DNA."

She scrambled through the photos, the sight of them resurrected Natosha's foul odor from within her subconscious. Christy blocked out the gory images. After skimming through the lab reports, she had to agree that it was of no benefit. The prints that were lifted belonged to the dead girl. Needless to say, the detective was back at square one. Linda foreman's results hadn't come back yet, but if the killer didn't leave any evidence at Natosha Little's home, chances were he covered his tracks at Linda Foreman's scene as well. As far as the diary she cuffed as a trump card, it held nothing of value.

The detective put the results away without peeling her eyes from the envelope. Her body language was now that of defeat; her dad wore the same look of failure before he died. "Where do I go from here?"

"Start over, refocus," the sergeant uttered, trying to restore motivation. "Don't think about where you go from here, concentrate on where you haven't been, the questions you never asked, maybe the things you overlooked." He snapped his fingers together, marinating in deep thought. "Natosha and Brenda Webb, perhaps they knew the killer. Natosha probably wasn't a random target. This individual plotted on her."

Brainstorming helped Christy see the picture from a clearer prospective. A combustion of new ideas entered her mind. "Yeah, he came back to murder the old lady out of the fear that she saw something, knew something, or could lead us into the right direction."

"That's the confidence of a natural investigator," he said, grinning. "And Linda Foreman, maybe she also knew the killer. He could have been a past fling or someone that her boyfriend knew or someone that she may have mentioned to him. Who knows? Go check the guy out."

The detective bobbed her head up and down in agreement. Sgt. Neal hit it right on the nose, sharpening her view. But Brenda Webb's murder was just as important as Natosha and Linda's, that's if all three were connected to the same perpetrator. She also made a mental note to question Brenda's husband. "Sgt. Neal, I truly appreciate all of your suggestions, but what about Chance and Miles? I don't want them stagnating my investigation."

"Okay, I'll call them off for the time being," he said, not really sure if it was the best idea. "As of this moment, all labs, reports, photos, and evidence will be at your disposal."

She gave a smile, swearing at Chance and Miles in her mind. Exclusively working the three cases were vital to apprehending the killer. She couldn't thank the sergeant enough.

Her welcome was returned by the soft smile that lifted his cheeks. "Well, then," Sgt. Neal directed his focus to the clock on the wall of his office, "you're still on a time limit. Get out of here," he ordered, fixing his tie.

Watching him transform back into an asshole, she rendered a solute, completely respecting that tough image he strove to uphold. The detective was used to being kicked out of his office, but this time she was anxious to depart.

Soon as the door closed, Sgt. Neal picked up his phone and made a call.

An enthusiastic voice answered on the second ring, "Detective Miles speaking."

"You already know who this is."

"Yeah, what's going on, SERGEANT NEAL?"

"I'm pulling you and Chance off that Brenda Webb case."

"Why?" he let out a sly chuckle. "It was just getting good."

"Never mind the reason," he shut the detective down. "I still want you two to process that scene, but turn everything in to me, understood!"

"Sure. I do what I'm told."

"Another thing..."

"I'm all ears."

"Keep an eye on Gatewood for me."

"Spy?"

"No, babysit, but keep your distance. She's in pursuit of a potentially dangerous suspect. Don't interfere with her investigation," Sgt. Neal instructed before abruptly hanging up.

* * * *

Still working the scene of Brenda Webb, Miles listened

to the phone go blank. Christy being provided with a cushion, that's the favor shit he was referring to. It just wasn't fair to him.

"Who was that?" Chance asked.

"Didn't you just hear me say Sgt. Neal when I was on the freaken phone... or didn't I say his name loud enough?" The reason he uttered the sergeant's name in the first place was to put his partner on point.

"Calm down, buddy. What ruffled your feathers?" was Chance's second question as Brenda's body was being cut down.

Miles bit at his lip, saying, "Sgt. Neal took us off this case, turning the investigation over to that cunt."

Chance instantly exploded, "That sonofabitch! I tell you... he's fucking her. Mark my words."

"But get this," Miles batted his eyes sardonically, "he also ordered us to babysit her."

"Unnnbeeelievable!"

The mood turned so somber that both men had to laugh just to keep from wanting to ring the sergeant's neck. Miles griped on, "I wanted so badly to tell him that we already have our orders for Gatewood."

"Damn it."

"Instead of getting in her way, we'll fall back, spy, not babysit. Let her screw herself."

Chance donned a stressful expression but tried to shelf it with a wise crack, "After this is over, I was thinking... maybe she wouldn't be a good exotic dancer, too bony. But she'd make a great crossing guard."

The two detectives ranted on, exchanging sour jokes, laughing until catching belly aches.

BOOK SEVENTEEN

The gossip of Brenda's demise sprawled throughout the hood like government cheese, but the word-to-mouth network circulated false information. By the time those rumors reached Danielle, the facts were completely inside out. The story Danielle heard was that Brenda and Tod got into a heated argument. Drunk off of some old-fashioned moonshine, Tod grabbed a knife and ran the blade through his wife's neck. What affected Danielle the most was she just seen Brenda, and that quick, in the blink of an eye, she was dead. First Natosha, now Brenda, both tragedies occurring back to back.

Danielle was still in bed. She and Paul slept through the morning, that was until being disturbed by an Avon customer tattling about the latest news. Though Danielle's feet had yet to touch the floor, the early afternoon appeared gloomy. Paul was resting on his back, belly protruding like a beach ball, snoring and chewing imaginary food. The vibration of Paul's snores were identical to a chainsaw, especially when he shifted gears. Danielle couldn't tolerate the racket, so much so that she threw blows at the man on many nights. But at the present, deep concentration prevented her from using his belly for a punching bag. Her eyes were staring at the television, mind someplace else.

She had a right to be a worrywart, now more so than ever, considering the circumstances. Danielle was so broke that she didn't have a single bill to put towards her daughter's funeral. If that wasn't enough to dampen the spirit, nothing was. She couldn't turn to Paul; he was also indigent, just as penniless as her. The mother considered going door-to-door to collect donations, but she was certain no one in her community had funds to spare. For one, April was on its last leg, and the end of the month was when famine struck most poor families. The few people she labeled as friends were having a difficult time taking care of their own children.

Since Danielle was unable to provide the best life for her daughter, at least she wanted to give Natosha a decent burial. Had Natosha bumped her head and drowned while swimming at a public pool, sympathizers would have come together to dispense money for the funeral, but it was a waste to pitch in for someone who took their own life. Danielle's community was more apt to abandon those who have already defeated themselves. Besides, suicide was the most sinful form of self-sacrifice. Before committing it, the mother felt Natosha should have took care of her own funeral expenses, rather than leave that burden on others to foot the bill.

[BUUUUUAAARRB...]

A disrespectful fart escaped out of Paul's ass. A silent one followed.

[ppphoooow...]

"You a nasty excuse fa ah man," Danielle muttered while clenching her fist. Instead of lunging at the fat fool, she decided to retreat before his rotten-egg aroma turned the room into a gas chamber. Danielle leapt out of the bed and took a stroll downstairs. As stated, minus the inability to finance Natosha's funeral, one other thing ate at her, which was the last words Brenda relayed about seeing someone running from Natosha's back door. The information seemed irrelevant at the time, but, perhaps, that incident should have been reported to the cops. She understood the hearsay was that Brenda died by the hands of her own husband, but Danielle still believed her death had something to do with their last conversation. However, in essence, she had no way in tying the two. So much was unfolding at such a fast pace.

Danielle opened a downstairs closet to remove Carlos from his cage. Instead of the mutt greeting her with a bark, the cage was empty, instantly putting Danielle on alert. She recalled stuffing Carlos inside of his cage before turning in last night, and Paul hadn't exited the bed, not even for a bathroom break... or did he? Maybe she was going crazy. Danielle's heart walloped in her chest, closing the closet's door and calling out for Carlos.

She searched his favorite hiding place under the couch. He wasn't there either. That's when Danielle panicked. She continued to look around, but the pup was nowhere to be found.

BOOK EIGHTEEN

By the time Christy got to the hospital, Tod had already passed away. Now it was only two who knew how his wife died—that was Brenda and the killer. While observing a moment of silence for the deceased couple, the detective sped over to the Baltimore City Jail. Weighing how to approach Linda's babyfather, rather than pull him out on a writ, she chose to register as a visitor. Using her ID to bypass regular restrictions, Christy wanted to speak with the man heart-to-heart. Considering the situation, Rodney already lost his freedom by getting arrested, so he probably wasn't in a mood to cooperate with any officer. In lieu of abusing authority to intimidate him, presenting herself as a concerned friend was a technique capable of producing favorable results.

Rodney was housed in a part of the jail called stealside. Its waiting room was small and moldy. Chairs were tightly arranged, leaving little legroom. Smirched tile was saturated with the strong scent of ammonia, yet the place still reeked of mildew. From where Christy was seated, she surmised that the actual visiting room was divided into three sections. The section to her immediate left had a slender hallway that split into two sides. A bullet-proof glass, mounted atop a long counter, separated protective custody and segregation inmates from loved ones.

The center visiting room resembled a horseshoe, thus gaining its attribute as such. In that sector, a double-grated grille substituted bullet-proof glass. This thick grille not only enforced the prohibition of physical contact but its tiny, grimy crevices were so cluttered that it presented a visual impossibility to piece together occupants on either side.

The final visiting room was reserved for legal advisors and law officials. This area to the far right was secured with two-sided booths. Though a thin glass partition served as a divider, set aside from the other aggressive designs, it included a small opening used to exchange legal paperwork from one side to the other. Most of the time, as a cruel ritual, lawyers were seated in these booths for extended periods, all in the name of waiting for their client to arrive. Refusing to go over the call of duty, correctional officers paged the inmate once. For the amount of time it took an inmate to travel from one point to another, this sluggish process was solely at that prisoner's discretion. The visitor had no choice but to endure the wait. Christy was no exception to the rule. As quickly as she wanted to get her little interrogation over with, it would take time. Patience was the key.

She was assigned a booth with that reality in mind. Once inside, an uncomfortable chill rattled her bones. Rubbing her hands together like two pieces of wood, she sat, placing her purse close. She surveyed the glass booth, eyes ricocheting off of every nook and cranny. Catching whim of a dusty cobweb just above her head, she dodged as though it was occupied. A thorough evaluation resulted in her opinion that the forsaken web was once the property of a spider who had long migrated. She lightly tapped the thin glass that would isolate her from Rodney. To her nearsighted delight, it was clear as looking through a fresh glass of water. She fetched a napkin from her purse to sanitize the counter. After making the area satisfactory, she felt more at ease.

With a sidelong glance, Christy scrutinized the few lawyers who utilized booths down from hers. Being that each space was soundproof, the discussion shared between crook and counsel remained confidential. She thought hard over the appropriate questions to ask Rodney. His criminal history or current charge didn't matter. Her only concern was if he could provide the golden brick needed to build a strong case or identify Linda's killer. Christy solicited a group of questions in her mind and placed them on speed dial. Ten minutes into chronologically detailing her thoughts, she was still alone in the booth. To keep herself from becoming impatient, Christy pulled out the diary and began to read:

As those wounds transformed before my eyes, I was subdued by a strange rage. Stranded someplace between joy and pain, the enigma-

"Hold up, that's not where I stopped," Christy whispered while turning the page. Zipping through a few paragraphs, words were scanned until finding the last thing she remembered:

my bone snapped.
"AHHHHHH!" I screamed as my arm dangled, blackin' out. It's crazy 'cause after my hospital stay, I was absent outta school fa a full month. Doctor said I broke my arm at da elbow. Staff treated me real nice. Den there were these people who came in ta ask if I was bein'

abused at home. If I was, dey could help. Dat was just a trick ta throw me in na system and mommy in jail—a method da government used ta break up da family. Mommy stayed at my bedside fa support, cryin' and constantly repeatin' how sorry she was fa whippin' me.

Told da man I fell off da bed and broke my arm. I knew dat was farfetched 'cause he believed different.

"Natosha," he said, "we're only here to help."

"Mister, whoever you said ya name was, I already told chu what happened." After he saw I wasn't gonna crack, he left my room.

When I did get back da school, it was fun. My whole class drew cartoon characters and sweet phrases all ova my cast. Even Ms. Denise drew da only sad face. Me and her knew da true pain she caused, but I kept it ta my lonesome and let bygones be bygones. God taught me dat forgiveness was an answer ta prayer; enmity would only end up givin' me hard lines under my eyes at a young age. Ms. Denise felt my situation was one rooted in child abuse, and her face bore da sorrow of eva makin' dat call. I enjoyed lettin' her stew in guilt.

Dat situation was behind me, and da only thing on my mind was Troy. He was da only face I didn't see.

Everybody said he had death in na family and left town. It took a week fa me ta come ta grips wit dat. Some mornings I still rushed ta 7Eleven in hopes ta see him there waitin' fa me. Without him 'round, school wasn't da same. I even stopped likin' hot dogs.

Da more I prayed, da more it seemed everythin' changed. As my world came crumblin', someone up top decided ta knock down da projects. Public Housin' gave us an option ta stay ova east or move ova west. Mommy chose West Baltimore, relocatin' ta a small town house off of Fulton Avenue. Ms. Stacy stayed ova east, choosin' Dundalk. Two months before da buildings came down, I said good-bye ta Rose, believin' we would neva see each other again. We did exchange numbers ta stay in touch.

Me, mommy, and Mr. Paul settled into da new house, watchin' other inner-city projects get knocked down ova news stations. Dey were just tryna move da black people out, white people in. Dey felt like why should white people have ta travel downtown ta their favorite stores. Dey plan was ta put downtown in walkin' distance fa dem.

A whole year helped me adjust ta da new house. All my life we lived in an apartment da size of a box truck.

Now we actually had a set of steps in our home. Weird wasn't da word. All da sexin' mommy and Mr. Paul was doin', could tell dey enjoyed our new location. Just like always, da only thing I had was me and my Bible. Did speak ta Rose on da phone from time ta time, but she got so sick of me talkin' 'bout Troy. Rose labeled him da mystery man, and I kind of felt he was a mystery 'cause da way he disappeared outta my world.

Besides school and runnin' earnings ta da store, I had no social life. Mommy started ta believe me bein' sixteen and so energetic, it was unhealthy not ta have any associates except Rose who was now just a phone buddy. So Mr. Paul went out and surprised me wit a dog. What frightened me was dat he brought da animal home wit blood all ova his fur. I asked him what happened?

He said, "The damn momma attacked me when I tried to grab it... but I got him dough."

Me and mommy laughed our heads off. Come ta find out, Mr. Paul crept ova a fence ta take da poor creature out of someone's yard. Dat momma dog waited fa da right moment da strike, and tore his butt up. He was lucky ta make it back ova dat fence alive. Claim he did it all fa me. I washed da puppy and named him Carlos. Took care of dat damn thing da way Mrs. Mary took care of me. I held Bible classes wit Carlos and took him fa daily walks. He was a blast until he wouldn't stop poopin' on our floor. When mommy started dislikin' Carlos, I wanted ta teach him da same lesson I taught Richard, but Mr. Paul begged us ta give da dog some time ta work it out. Dat's what we did. After gettin' his brains beat out enough wit newspaper, I guess Carlos caught on.

One evenin' after school, I received a call from Rose. She was all excited, shoutin' into da phone, "Girrrl, you wouldn't believe who I ran into!"

I was doin' my homework, already playin' da guessin' game wit a slew of multiple choice questions, now she wanted me ta play da same game wit her. Exhausted, I just said, "Who?"

"I ran into my cousin Lester."

Da sound of his name gave me a sour taste, though I neva shared wit her da situation dat happened between me and him. Still responded, "Okay, no big deal. Don't you already see him enough..."

"Girl, shut it up," she said while laughin'. "Me seeing him ain't the main topic I'm tryna get across to you."

I heard her inhale deeply.

"Lester's friend has a little brother who has a friend and-"

I interrupted, "Let me see if I got dis right, Lester's brother got a friend who got a brother."

"Noooooo. Listen. Lester's friend has a brother who has a friend. Anywhoz, my cousin was ova his friend Chuck house. He overheard Chuck's little brother, Travon, talking to his friend 'bout some girl named Natosha."

"So." I said while tryna figure out where our conversation was goin'. "It's a bunch of Natosha's in dis world."

"Travon's friend was talking 'bout how Tosha was his first love and how he would do anything to find her, all this whoop-de-whoop."

"Rose, what's da point?"

"Daaaah point is that Travon's friend name is Troy, and the Natosha he's crying over is you!"

I dropped da house phone. I could still hear Rose on da line...

[Tosha! Tosha! Tosha!]

My head exploded. Everythin' inside of me said I was daydreamin'. There was no way such a coincidence was happenin' ta me. I picked up da phone, "Hello-"

"Hello, Tosha, did you come back to earth yet?"

My voice trembled, "I'm here."

"If you're freaked out 'bout that, this is really going to blow your mind. Guess what else?"

"What?"

Rose anxiously continued, "I told Lester to invite Troy over my house this weekend. Said I'm having a dope party."

"Your mova gonna zap out on you."

She replied, "My mother is going out of town to gamble. You know how she do. Sooooo, I'll have this pad all to myself. The question is-"

I read her mind... "Yeah, how am I gonna get my mova ta let me come ova there."

"BINGO!"

"Don't worry 'bout dat. I'll figure somedin out, even if I gotta run away."

"You serious?" asked Rose, soundin' a bit concerned.

"Syke. You know I'm just playin'." We both snickered at da same time. "I'll cover dis end wit me and my mova. You just make sure Troy is there," I said jokingly, yet in a demandin' way.

"I got this," she guaranteed.

We spent da rest of da time on da line talkin' 'bout how good God was and how he worked in mysterious ways.

It was four days shy of da weekend. If I was gonna get mommy ta agree, I had ta start doin' small things now ta butter her up, which I did. Before Friday came 'round, I informed mommy dat Rose's church was throwin' a gospel summit. It was gonna be a two-day event, so I had ta be ova Rose's house by Friday fa early Saturday mornin' ta attend both services. Assumin' she was doin' somedin slick, she said I couldn't go ova on Friday ta stay, but I could go on Saturday and be back on Sunday. Pretended havin' a little attitude but really wanted ta smile.

On dat night I packed my bag and rushed fa da weekend ta come. When it did, Rose agreed ta meet me at a bus stop down Lexington Market. Dagether, we would travel ta her house. Da plan was executed like clockwork. I was at Rose's house in no time. When I placed my bag down on her couch, reality struck. Us two screamed like we was watchin' a scary movie. It was a rush of excitement.

It's been foreva since we seen each other and we had da whole house ta ourselves. On top of dat, if everything went right, I was 'bout ta have one of my deepest prayers come true. Dat prayer was ta bring me and Troy back dagether. Rose and I spent half da day decidin' what ta wear out of her closet. I chose dis cute sundress. It looked better on me den her. We even played in Ms. Stacy's makeup, puttin' a light foundation on my face.

Lester was bringin' Troy ova by seven. When I finally heard da doorbell, me and Rose ran in circles, even bumpin' into each other. When we raced ta Rose's room, she hid me under da bed, hurryin' downstairs. Butterfly's invaded my tummy; I was so nervous. Not knowin' what was goin' on, I stayed in da blind fa a couple of minutes, dat was until I heard footsteps comin' up da stairs. Den I heard Rose.

"We are having a party... the crowd just haven't come yet."

Da male's voice sounded disappointed, "Lester said this spot was going to be off the hook! What's up with that?"

"Trust me," Rose spoke convincingly, "it will be. I

just need you to help me get something out of my room."
When Rose's door came open, I put my hands ova my mouth
ta stop from screamin'. I could clearly see Rose's
feet. She didn't have on shoes, but beside her feet
stood a fresh pair of boots. Couldn't see anything
above da ankles, but I could feel Troy's presence. Da
next thing I heard was Rose giggle. I knew her long
enough ta know what dat meant—she was up ta somedin.
"Troy, let's start off by lifting up this bed."
My heart almost pounded a hole through da floor. I
removed both hands from my mouth ta place dem ova my
eyes. I felt da bed disappear from behind me. In came a
light draft. Da room got completely silent. I could
feel Troy hoverin' ova me in awe, most likely tryna
figure out who was da girl facedown on da floor.
Before Troy could express himself, Rose said, "I want
to introduce you to a friend of mine. Troy this is
Natosha, and, Tosha, this is Troy."
I lifted my head ta see his sexiness standin' ova me.
He was in all black, face trimmed neatly.
"Tosha..." he paused in a speechless effort.
Rose already made me feel like Eve when God found Adam
and her hidin' behind a bush. Since my cover was blown,

I stood, knees bucklin', also at a loss of words.

"Baby," he broke da silence, "thought I'd never find you."

As I looked him in da eyes, he grabbed me close and planted a juicy kiss. I opened my lips ta give him access ta my tongue.

"Ooookay, let me give you two lovebirds some privacy," said Rose, leavin' da room and closin' da door.

I didn't even pay Rose any mind. My eyes were now shut as I experienced da most intimate thing dat eva happened ta me.

"Tosha, I missed you so much."

"I missed you, too," I whispered back as he continued ta kiss me. Didn't even care ta ask where he'd been. Da only thing dat mattered is he was wit me now. My mind went back ta da day my mova beat me and dat promise I made ta myself. Since den, I knew dat Troy would be my first and last. Now I was in Rose's room, her mova gone, me and Troy finally alone. Da timin' could not been more perfect.

"Did you truly miss me," he asked, caressin' my body.

"I missed you so much dat I saved myself fa you," were da words dat slipped out. Swear I didn't mean ta say dat. Troy turned me ta face da bed, forcin' my palms against da mattress as if I was 'bout ta get frisked.

"We're meant for each other. The Lord brought us back together, this time for good," he said.

Troy was da driver, me da passenger. As dem busy hands knew exactly where he was 'bout ta take us, I was just so anxious ta get there. He slowly lifted da rear of my dress, breathin' becomin' heavier behind me. My virgin muscles throbbed in anticipation.

"Tosha," he sucked on my ear, "it's all 'bout us from this point on."

Not only was his hands massagin' my backside but his words were also makin' love ta my mind. I was willin' ta give every part of myself ta him. Da sharp arch of my lower back was no more than a gesture of submission. He read my body well, leanin' my head forward as my panties came down. Troy eased his finger down da crack of my rump, manipulatin' my private area.

"Woooow, you're soaked, and it's tight."

I moaned while feelin' his finger dig knuckle-deep inside my cotton candy. Strangely, experienced more pleasure than pain. Sticky discharge escaped my body, oozin' all ova his fingers. Da temperature of da room *heightened.*

"Baby," Troy muttered while lickin' da back of my neck,
"we don't have to do this if you don't want to. I'll
wait until you're ready. I'm not going anywhere."

"Troy, I'm yours. We don't have ta wait... we already
waited long enough," I said, feelin' his finger diggin'
deeper.

"Okay, bend over a little more," he instructed, pullin'
me at da waist.

I pushed my backside out further as he fumbled wit da
front of his jeans. Once his penis made contact, my
virginity no longer existed. He tore me apart fa what
seemed like forever, fillin' me wit his hot seed. Me
and Troy was now consummated, and dat was da first day
of da rest of my life.

What Christy just read had her swimming in her seat.
She felt like a pervert by letting herself get worked up
over the story of two children. With herself still being
sexually inexperienced at twenty-eight years of age, even
that was surreal. The only time she touched herself was for
hygienic purposes. Christy couldn't miss what she never
had. Besides the scoop on Natosha's first sexual

145

extravaganza, the diary was like reading a soap opera. The girl had her mother believing she was such a good cookie but was sneaking around with this guy, Troy, the whole time, which established a propensity for deception. Christy decided to find Rose because her victim's best friend knew a side of her no one else did. Ultimately, she also had to locate this Troy, but, in the meantime, she would prioritize and deal with first things first. The nearest goal on her agenda was to speak with Rodney.

She'd been patiently waiting for nearly an hour. The detective was about to demand that the inmate be paged a second time until she noticed an older fellow strutting her way. He passed the occupied booths, instinctively zeroing in on her. Maybe common sense directed him to her, probably because she was the only person sitting alone. The guy looked a decade older than Linda. An athletic physique didn't fit his chubby face. He appeared as the type forced to stay in shape due to health reasons. To a woman with low expectations, he wasn't hard on the lids. Christy imagined him being far from Linda's type, but beauty was in the eyes of the beholder.

On the opposite side of the glass divider, he cracked the door just enough to peer in. "You ain't mah lawyer,"

Rodney said, patting an itchy scalp beneath fresh cornrows.

She flashed her badge at the man, ensuring that he was in the right booth. "Hello. My name is Christy Gatewood, and I am a detective with the Baltimore Homicide Unit. I'd like to speak with you."

Scowling, he disapproved, "Sorry, Detective, but I ount do no talkin' without mah lawyer."

She challenged his frown with a chummy smile. Aiming to establish a clear understanding, Christy made her intentions known, "You're not being rebooked on a new charge. Frankly, I'm not interested in the facts of your current case. It's none of my business."

"Dig dis," sporadic hand gestures aided his words, "I'm ah real street nigga. You's ah police. Dat's apples and beans. We ain't even in tha same fruit family. In otha words," he beamed at her with a frozen stare, "we got nothin' in common. Less you gonna slide me ah key to tha gate, I'm peace out."

He and she were at a stalemate. His guards went up the moment that faint light in the booth caught the gleam of her badge. "You're right," Christy agreed with his point of view, "we are from two different worlds, but there's one thing you're wrong about..."

"Sho' ya right-"

"We do have something in common."

"Doubt dat."

"It's Linda Foreman," uttered Christy, watching the ice in his eyes slowly melt. "Are you aware that she was found yesterday-"

Rodney jumped in with his attitude on full throttle, "Yeah, heard 'bout it when I called uptown dis mornin'. So what... y'all think I had somethin' to do wit it?"

"No, I don't." Christy eliminated him as a suspect. She knew the difference between a person with something to hide and a thick-skinned individual shielding emotional pain. Rodney was the latter. "Quite often, when it comes to these cases, we normally consult with the victim's partner and family. They're investigated to see if alibis check out. As for you, you're already behind bars, so I know you had nothing to do with it; however, maybe you can direct me to the right path."

"Tha right path... what chu mean? No one knew dis would happen. Life wasn't nat bad. Loved her tha same way she loved me, my fuckin' rowdog. Still can't understand why she did dat and left our son behind." His knees almost gave way, but Rodney caught himself before the shift in his equilibrium took control.

Christy was studious in the science of body language; therefore, she recommended he take a seat. Conceding resistance, he fancied her suggestion. The detective took advantage of his weakest moment, "I'm terribly sorry for your loss. To be completely honest, Ms. Foreman's death has yet to be ruled a homicide, but I'm investigating it as one. There's reason to believe she was murdered."

That incited Rodney. "Is dat right?"

Christy didn't want his defenses to go back up. "Calm down. This is only preliminary data, no concrete evidence. That's why I'm here."

"Lady, when I touch down, if somebody killed mah son's mutha, I'm comin' back to prison for tha rest of mah life!" Rodney adamantly swore.

His initial response was normal, nothing to hold against him. Had he not reacted in such a manner, that would have generated a question mark; nevertheless, anger offered no solution. "I know it's unfair to pour this on you all at once, but I need you to put everything aside and think rational."

Rodney did an excellent job taming his tears. Shaking off the shock, he drew a deep breath and said, "I'm good now. What can I help you wit?"

Christy asked a series of questions within a thirty minute period, which yielded not one promising lead, but she listened on...

"Lin was upset tha last we spoke. She said some asshole cop pulled her over and was real touchy feely."

Christy didn't buy it. Though she took it as a lie, personally concluding that that was Rodney's way in lashing out at authority; still and all, Christy played along only to see how far it would stretch. "Did Linda provide any additional information about the officer: his name, unit number, or even a description?"

"No. Well, I was supposed to call her back, but dis stupid jail went on lock over ah stabbin'. Couldn't get to tha phone till dis mornin'. Ah relative told me 'bout tha news."

Christy pawned off those touchy-feely allegations. "I'll look into what you say she said."

Rodney went into a panic attack. "I need to get tha fuck outta here for I go crazy! Lin was all I had. Now mah son is out there without ah mutha or fartha. If you can get me outta here, I'll help find dis muthafucka!" He banged the adjoining table with his fist.

That unrehearsed action startled the detective, but she kept it smooth. "I can only imagine how you feel, but I'm really on top of this matter. The case is in good hands," she said, sliding her card through the small opening at the bottom of the glass. "Even if it's collect, call me if you think of anything else."

Rodney studied the card, looking at the name. As if trying to trap a wild thought, he sneered, "Dis say your last name Gatewood..."

She gave an inquisitive expression. "Correct. I identified myself when I showed my badge."

That's when he recalled the thought, "Naw... naw, tha Gatewood I'm talkin' 'bout is ah detective dat work Robbery."

The fact she used to work in that division made Christy especially curious. "I used to be a robbery detective but transferred to Homicide."

"Is dat guy, can't think of his name," Rodney's eyes almost rolled into the back of his skull, "might be Ronald Gatewood... Rolland Gatewood, somethin' like dat?"

The conversation took a twist.

"Do you mean Raymond Gatewood?" she lobbed, eyes squinting.

"Yeah, dat's tha name! Was he any kin to you?"

Christy didn't know whether or not to be honest. Integrity made her answer the question in truth, "Yes, that was my father."

"Oh, you tha daughta. Damn, dat's even betta," he wore a wry smile, "if you got some friends in high places, considerin' where you used to work, me havin' ah robbery charge, maybe you can pull some strings."

"Yes, I do have some powerful friends," she confirmed, "but why should I ask them to bend the same law they'd risk their lives to uphold? If I considered the thought, how could I benefit?"

"I got some exclusive info 'bout cha pops."

The detective was now at the edge of her seat. "Alright, keep talking."

"Check dis out," here came the disclaimer, "I'm far from ah rat, but mah back against tha wall. I don't need no games."

"Understandable."

"Now, if you give me your word to make somethin' shake, I'll put chu down wit some serious shit," he claimed with arms folded, leaning back in his seat.

If all she had to do was give her word for this convict

to grease her ears, when the law stated anything he said could and would be used against him in court, pitching a false promise held no weight. "If you swear to tell me all you know about this so-called secret info," her expression was now as solid as a brick wall, "you have my word that I'll try to see what I can do."

The detective seemed like a pretty fair person, the best he'd seen behind the badge. Though it was no way to be certain, Rodney took his chances. He slowly scooted forward and whispered, "I had ah bunky who came over tha jail for ah new trial. He did most of his time out Jessup, but dat was till tha courts vacated his life sentence."

"Did your bunky have a name?"

He overworked his neck with a shake of the head. "Can't tell you dat 'cause I count want mah name to pop up in nothin'. I'm just puttin' you down wit what's in tha air, but, for tha sake of argument, we'll just call him Weezy."

"I can accept that," Christy uttered, hoping not to discourage him. It was best to shut her mouth and open up her ears.

"Me and mah bunky was suppa tight. We'd eat togetha, get high togetha, and even go to war togetha, all of dat. Anyway, he was good friends wit tha dude who murdered your pops."

None of it sat well with Christy, but she didn't wear her feelings in the opening.

Rodney continued, "Tha dude who was sentenced to ninety years for dat murder, he got chopped up for somethin' unrelated. But he told Weezy ah mouthful 'bout someone paid him to wipe your pops down."

Just the thought of it stung her, but Christy wanted to be sure she heard him right. "A murder-for-hire?"

"Yeah, ah hit. Yo told Weezy tha contract wasn't given by just some average joe, it was by anotha police officer."

The booth got totally silent.

Christy already had her own beliefs about an unseen enemy, but who paid someone to kill her father? If what Rodney said was fact, what was this crooked officer trying to cover up? The detective couldn't let the thug see her as an emotional wreck. "Is that it?"

"Yeah, dat's all Weezy shared wit me. He didn't say what tha hit was for."

Her next sentence came out sharp and clear, "Okay, thank you for the information; it's time for me to leave." Christy stood and cuffed her purse, darting out of the booth.

"Hey! Hey!" shouted Rodney. "What 'bout what chu supposed to do for me?"

"Standby," she shouted back in an echo.

BOOK NINETEEN

Chance smacked his partner's arm. "Heads up, we got movement!"

Miles was abruptly snatched out of his catnap. "Goddamnit, you motherfucker, scared the shit out of me."

"Look." Chance pointed to Christy marching westward.

"Calm the hell down," Miles quickly put the binoculars to his eyes, "I see her."

Not even twenty yards from the Baltimore City Jail, the pair were parked on Eager Street in an unmarked vehicle. The distance was close enough to provide a clear line of sight, yet far enough not to hatch suspicion. As she hopped in her car, Miles observed Christy place a cellular device to her ear.

* * * *

She answered the phone with an apparent attitude, "Hello."

"Is something wrong?" Tony asked, feeling the tension.

"No, it's nothing I can't handle," she responded, lightly gassing the peddle. Aborting the small talk,

156

Christy informed him that now wasn't a good time, urging he call back later.

"I just need to borrow a minute; I'll pay you back with interest."

That was a sweet line, one of enchantment had she not been so stressed. Since he was trying to be so nice, Christy toned down her aggression. "Minute granted."

Tony thought his voice was the reason she got upset. "I apologize again for running out on you. I still owe you a date."

"Told you, you don't owe me anything."

"Then what about the minute you just lent me?"

As polite as she could, Christy uttered, "Tony, I'm not up for the word game. What's going on?"

"I want to see you," he bluntly stated.

She intercepted his advance, "Not now."

"Why?"

"Because I'm on my way home to hit the sack."

"It's great you mentioned home because I was thinking about coming to your spot to catch a movie and some takeout."

He was determined to spend time with her. Maybe that was his way in attempting to lift her spirits. "Say we did hookup, it wouldn't be at my place," she retorted, envisioning the messy apartment.

"Oh, my bad, just figured your comfort zone would be the pick of the litter. No matter where we meet, it'll work for me. I really need to see you," he insisted, saying whatever possible to carry out his promise to It.

Christy refused to go back and forth. He obviously was motivated to insert himself into her world. Tony's determination was cute, potentially what she needed to break the monotony. With all that was on her mind, maybe she didn't need to be alone. A friendly gathering wouldn't hurt. After processing the thought of it, for the first time, Christy gave directions to her pad, setting the rendezvous for 9:00 p.m.

Their dialogue concluded with smiles on both ends.

The detective drove herself home, this time paying no attention to the rearview mirror. Not only daydreaming about Tony, her mind was still overwhelmed with the information Rodney imparted. But as a jailbird, his creditability was no prize. One in desperate need of assistance would lie to God with a straight face. When Christy made detective, the first rule she learned was that there's no honor amongst thieves, robbers, lawyers, or mechanics. However, what if Rodney was telling the truth? What if he did come across someone who had the real scoop behind her father's death? It was a rookie mistake to shirk data before investigating the facts. Bombarded by the suicide cases, now also carrying the weight of a fresh discovery concerning her dad, there was too much on her plate at once. With the lower compartment of the hourglass swiftly filling, if a miracle didn't happen by the end of the following day, her current position was history.

Christy, as a creature of habit, parked and went straight to the mailbox. While surfing through coupons, she unheeded the unmarked vehicle whipping into the lot.

* * * *

"So, this is where the cunt lives," uttered Chance, watching her disappear into an apartment building. "She's right in the heart of Jewville."

Miles offered a cheap smirk. "This is a nice community, reckon she can afford it with only herself as an expenditure. Selfish bitch. Jewville is a perfect place for a female so tight up the ass."

Chance snickered. "That ass wouldn't come your way if

you was the last peter on earth."

He momentarily became drunk with laughter. "If Sgt. Neal can bang it, I'm sure I could."

Chance discounted his statement, "In your dreams, bud."

"Wet dreams."

"You're pathetic."

Miles got a kick out of Chance's look of disgust, then he sobered up. "Um-mmmmm, she's not worth the headache. Bless the clown who'd stoop that low to deal with a cunt so self-centered."

"I mean, who cares about her personal life, anyway?"

"Not we," Miles declared.

"Or the captain."

"Yeah, that's why he entrusted us to derail her career. Sgt. Neal turned Gatewood into a suicide detective. Whatever information she has is classified, a love secret between him and her."

"That is so unprofessional," Chance remarked.

"They can shine now, but it won't be long before the facts, if there's any, become public information. It don't take an astronaut to decipher the only defendant of a blatant suicide is the idiot who killed himself. All that talk about Gatewood chasing some dangerous suspect, it's a bowl of crap, something to stall time. The only thing she's chasing is her own shadow. I bet she has nothing concrete, besides her own speculation, to support any pursuit."

"The point is," Chance unbuttoned his blazer, "it doesn't matter. Whatever Gatewood's chasing, we have only until tomorrow night to keep that carrot on a rope and out of her possession. We gave Capt. Dagger our word."

Miles snorted boastfully as though the mission was already completed. "Ummp, favors..."

"...Ass kissing."

"Or blue-collar credit... a shortcut straight to the top. Soon we'll be the ones behind the desk, jerking our cocks, calling the shots."

Chance sipped from a cup of cold coffee. "So true. Can't wait."

"Oh, and while we're on the topic of favors," Miles reclined his seat, "do me a solid and give a tap if you see anything worthwhile."

"Patted you the last time-"

"No, you smacked my freaken arm when I was just about to grope Chaka Khan."

"You say her of all people?" Chance heard enough, adjusting his own seat to a relaxed position. "You really

161

need to get laid."

"I will soon as your wife stops being so stingy."

"Cool. Screwed yours last night."

"Thanks. Better you than me."

Chance allowed him the last word.

* * * *

Danielle confronted Paul after thoroughly searching for the dog, "So what chu sayin', Carlos busted out da cage himself, just ran off, huh?"

"I'm not sayin' ah damn thing, but what I know is I ain't do nothin' wit da li'l nigga."

She maintained her own suspicions. Paul had to be the one who crept out of bed in the wee hours and cut Carlos loose. That was the only plausible explanation. Since Natosha was gone, Carlos was the only stumbling block that stood in the way of Paul having her all to himself. "You just so selfish, man. Looks ugly on you."

"You da ugliest one," he responded.

She swung at Paul.

He blocked, rolling out of the bed. "Dat's the problem wit chu now, woman. Can neva keep those claws ta yourself.

What chu need da do is fight dat attitude of yours."

"Guy, if you don't get da hell outta my face and find my dog, you gonna really think I'mz ah crazy bitch!"

"Chill out," he lowered his voice, "we just under ah lotta stress dis second. Steal ah breath, and let's start ova wit ah betta attitude. Ready, set, go," Paul paused, closed his jaundice-ridden eyes, took in as much oxygen as humanly possible, and exhaled slowly. He repeated this self-appointed process three times. "Now... dat's betta. So, how you doin'?"

She threw a pillow at him. "You look sooooo stupid right now. We fightin'. What I look like closin' my eyes durin' a fight? Lucky I ain't bop you when you closed yours."

"Still poppin' dem gums." Paul did a little sidestep, which was his own version of the Electric Slide. "Give me ah smooch, and I'll do anything you want."

Danielle tried not to smile. Aside from the stupidity that made her pity Paul, she sustained a bounteous love for him as the result of mastering how to deal with her. Danielle's over-the-top attitude was what chased Natosha's father away, but her Paul was like no other.

He held out his hairy arms. "Come on, woman, kick it

163

out... don't make me come ova there and take mine."

Danielle turned her face away, toiling to hide her teeth.

The fat man knew his woman and how to break down her defenses. "Dat's it. I'm comin' in hot." Like a bear, he rushed to Danielle's side and wrapped his arms around her.

"Make me sssick," she said, rewarding him with a kiss.

"We gonna get through dis as ah family, like we always have."

Those words of encouragement made Danielle bury her head into his chest. Her eyes were instantly drenched.

He compassionately whispered, "Now, how many times you gon cry?"

"I'ma keep on until Natosha come back home," Danielle whispered back through descending tears.

"She gone, woman."

"Don't wanna hear dat."

"It's the truth. Look," he lifted her chin, "the funeral home committed to givin' us ah fair price. Dem good folks know it's ah struggle out here. All we gotta do is wait for the medical examiner to let her body go."

"Why won't dey release it? Been two days."

"Can't answer dat. Dey probably still runnin' tests.

Keep in mind, dey said her body was so bad off dat the process would take time. Their delay give us time to come up wit ah plan to raise some green. Everything happens for ah reason."

Owing to the incomprehensible affair, Danielle's eyes blinked excessively as she blamed herself, "Should'a neva fought wit Tosha. If I just been grateful, my baby be alive."

"Didn't I just say everything happen for ah reason? Dis the lawd's plan. You and me should pray on it." Paul closed his eyes.

Danielle gave his face a love tap.

His lids sprung back open. "Hey, what was dat for?"

"Didn't I tell youuu neva close your eyes in a fight?"

He gave her a look of skepticism. "You ah special project."

"Ummm-hum," she snatched loose, "now go find my Carlos."

This time he obeyed.

BOOK TWENTY

If loneliness had an actual odor, the apartment was saturated with its bitter stench. Pondering Rodney's accusations, Christy tossed her purse, jacket, and shoulder holster onto the couch, rushing to her father's room. "Oh, Daddy, please forgive me for invading your belongings, but if there's something here you want me to know," she spoke into the air, twisting the doorknob east, "may your spirit guide me to it."

The door opened with a shrill cry. The illumination of an evening sky peeked through a slender crack beneath shutters, catching the contour of a 5" x11" inch picture frame on an end table. Christy glided over to the photo and picked it up. The images were that of herself, mother, and dad. She was an infant within the photo, cuddled in the arms of both parents. The three were smiling, representing a perfect portrait of love. Although the picture depicted happiness, a huge separation was underway. The exact cause of her parents' divorce remained a riddle. Christy hadn't heard from her mom ever since the courts granted Raymond custody. No birthday cards, holiday greetings, or visits to Christy's school. You'd think she never had a mother, which was hard to fathom because their bond was once inseparable before the court's decision.

A tear fell, splashing against the dusty glass covering. She pitched the wooden frame onto the bed and searched her father's personal effects. She shook out articles of clothing, raided pockets, and read through miscellaneous paperwork. Christy even located a 38. Special stashed within a shoe box. An hour into the hunt, she found nothing odd. Frustrated, she flipped into cleaning mode, making the rest of the apartment presentable. A refreshing shower followed the smashing of a potpie. Before climbing into the bed for a nap, the picture frame was switched from Raymond's room to her own dresser. It would keep Christy's company until her date arrived.

She jumped at the startling sound of an object dropping in the living room. The bedroom door was ajar though her surroundings were pitch black. Besides the crashing sound, the apartment was silent as a tomb. It could have been one of her African figurines that fell from the wall, worn-out adhesive caused them to do that from time to time. Semi-sleep, jarring thoughts came and went. She was reentering dreamland when a rattling sound stifled her journey. Panic rushed in as optimism rushed out. The clatter was too loud to be a rodent; someone was definitely inside of her home. Christy sat up in the bed, hearing the ruckus of an individual rummaging through her property. The detective's heart pounded with fright. Feeling around the night stand for her service weapon, she then remembered leaving it on the sofa.

"Shit," Christy inaudibly whispered, praying the intruder hadn't discovered it. Apparently, this person didn't know she was home and had yet to move into the back of her apartment. As a rule, she wouldn't make her presence known by shouting out threats. This wasn't the movies; the world she lived in was real. Remaining unseen would give her the leverage needed to gain the advantage. Using that thought as a strategy, she slowly slid out of bed, tiptoeing to the closet to retrieve a trophy baton that been with her since patrol. Evenly balancing herself upon both heels, she eased through the bedroom door. Peering down a dark hallway, she saw nothing, yet heard more rattling.

Holding the baton as a baseball bat, Christy moved along the dark passageway until witnessing a light ricocheting throughout the living room. The shoulder holster was visible from where she stood, appearing empty, meaning her service weapon was now in the hands of the intruder. The only other weapon in the apartment was the 38. Special. She had a better chance with that than bringing a stick to a gunfight. So, instead of continuing forward, she crept backwards to her dad's room. Before she got there, a swift figure leapt into the hallway.

Christy stopped in motion, lifting the baton. At the sight of her battle stance, the figure paused. After a couple of seconds, the figure stepped forward, outlined by the glow of a flashlight within its backdrop. Observing the figure's face scared Christy shitless. She dropped the baton and gasped. The face was Natosha's. It appeared the dead girl climbed out of the body litter, escaped from the medical examiner's office, and found her way straight to Christy's home. Natosha's face was bloated, skin shredded, infested with maggots. Her eyes were glued shut. Everything about Natosha spelled death. The hideous corpse slowly reached out, pointing the 9 mm. at her.

Christy parted her lips to scream—

[BUZZZZ! BUZZZZ! BUZZZZ!]
While punching on the mattress, she was awakened to the

doorbell. Violently falling onto the floor, it took Christy a moment to collect herself. Once realizing it was only a dream, she looked over at the clock reading 8:55 p.m.

[BUZZZZZZ! BUZZZZZZ!]

"Hold on! I'm coming!" she shouted though knowing her soft voice wouldn't carry three floors down. Using the nightgown to wipe sweat from her forehead, Christy dashed to the intercom. "Yes," she uttered sweetly, brushing her hair at the same time.

"Christy, it's me, Tony. I been down here buzzing you like crazy, thought I had the wrong apartment."

The intercom's loud volume tickled her eardrums. "I'm sorry. You're being buzzed up now." She pressed the entrance button and looked around the living room at everything still intact, even her service weapon was tightly fastened within its holster. Christy wished she got up thirty minutes earlier to tidy up by changing into something more presentable. It would be rude to turn the man away or make him wait any longer due to a lack of preparation on her part. As the footsteps of her date got louder, she cracked the front door and stood behind it, keeping it only wide enough to reveal the corner of her smile. Tony soon stood outside of her door. He was garbed in a fitted summer suit; its color was the exact pink matching the dozen of long-stem roses cuffed behind his back.

"Excuse my attire. I jumped out of bed," she said, closing the door once he stepped in.

"That's alright," he responded, secretly studying her shapely frame, "here... these are for you."

Christy grabbed the roses. "Awwww, they're so beautiful," she said with a pout. Coworkers had given her flowers before, most came pouring in on the anniversary of her father's death, but she never received roses, specially on an informal level. "You didn't have to go out of your way to get these."

He accepted the hug that came with the gift, lustfully holding her close. "That's nothing."

Christy had to peel herself out of his embrace. "Let me put these in some water."

"Be my guest-"

"No," said Christy, walking towards the kitchen, "you're my guest. Make yourself at home."

Tony made the couch his haven, noticing a shoulder holster beside him. To murder her without incident, he needed to get the weapon out of her reach. Tony joshed in a friendly tone, "Hey, do you just leave your gun laying around?"

She returned from the kitchen. "Naw, not usually."

"Bad, bad habit."

"I was so tired when I got in, shuuesh, I placed it there." Christy picked up the shoulder strap and excused herself, returning so fast that she forgot to slip some jeans on.

"I was about to start missing you," he jeered, loosening his tie.

"Oh, be quiet." She took a seat next to him. "You're the one who walked out on our date, but those flowers were a wonderful make-up gift. Thank you."

"Forget about those things. You're a beautiful flower, and tonight it's all about you," he muttered, gazing into her eyes.

Since this was the first time inviting someone into her home, she wanted everything to be perfect. Plus, Tony was on his game, saying and doing all the right stuff to make her feel enthused. His presence forced out that stench of loneliness; in fact, a ray of joy radiated from his charming aura. Christy took pleasure in Tony anointing her home with his harmonious spirit.

172

His eyes showed deep interest when he asked, "So, Christy, tell me a little about your day. What's been keeping you so busy?" He really wanted to know what progress she made in Natosha's case.

The detective responded by explaining small highlights. Her visit to the jail, the thoughts about her dad, the suicide murders, and the fact of working extra hard to save her career, those topics were left untouched. She'd been dealing with those matters around the clock, so, for the moment, Christy desired to replace them with brighter thoughts. Her date was correct, tonight was all about her. She continued to chat on...

Meanwhile, as she vented, the officer focused on nothing but the voice within his own head: *I know that pussy good. I can kill her now and hide the body between the pillows of this couch, or I can make it look like a suicide. Them damn lips*—So I went to headquarters, and dropped off a few things. You caught me right when I was finishing up. Wasn't expecting your call.—*I'd love for her to suck me off. Should I fuck the corpse? Nah, that wouldn't be much fun. I'll nail her while she's still alive, make her scream and beg*—I got in and done some cleaning. Ate a microwave pie—*for her life. Since she's*

173

going to die shortly, I'll take the pussy. No problem.

Without hearing a word of what she said, he cut in, "I know that's right. You've been a busy bug, even ate before I got here."

"Yes, but we can still order out if you'd like."

Ready to make a move, his nose began to sweat. "My taste buds aren't pinging at the moment."

She wanted to honor the plans he made over the phone. "What about the takeout? Now you have no appetite?"

"My only appetite is for you," he flatly uttered. Before his statement could resonate, Tony dived onto Christy and scuffled for a kiss.

She tried to push him up. "What the hell do you think you're doing?"

"I wanted to sniff your panties from the second I saw you. This pussy is mine, and I won't accept no." He forced her arms against the couch, locking down her hands.

As the assault progressed, she struggled under his weight. Christy fought to no avail. "Get the hell off of me!" she demanded, kicking her legs until they were spread open.

Loving the chase, Tony transformed into a wild animal. Lust and murder driven, he clamped her lips together by biting down with his teeth. The vice wasn't substantial enough to leave a mark, but it did serve its purpose in keeping her from screaming. Somehow, while all of this was going on, Tony managed to bind her hands using his tie. Once her limbs were no longer a threat, he released her lips and whispered, "Don't scream or I'll be forced to teach you a lesson. All I want is to make you feel good."

"You are an officer of the law. We arrest rapists. Why are you doing this to me?"

He responded by lifting her gown to expose a perky rack. His lips found her nipples, spanking both with his soft tongue.

Confused and frightened, she still purred under his control, totally turned on by his flesh against hers. He was completely out of line, but to be manhandled, conquered in this manner, made her vagina throb. With or without permission, she knew this was about to be her first sexual experience, an encounter she'd never forget.

BOOK TWENTY-ONE

Sgt. Neal stood inside the squad room, eyes canvassing a huge eraser board used to record the growing number of homicides each year. From January to April of 2006, the current number was already soaring at 197. However, records showed the numbers were at 141 the same time the year before. To date, 56 more bodies had fallen in the new calendar. Out of 197 fresh homicides, 88 were solved, leaving 109 cases open. The way Sgt. Neal viewed it, their division was losing the war in making the streets a playground, which meant more murderers were escaping the long arm of justice.

Out of thirty homicide detectives, dividing that number between three shifts, each shift maintained a total of ten split into teams of five. Sgt. Neal supervised the squadron Christy was assigned to. It was irrefutable that Chief Jorden had the values and structure of the division measured by difficult, unrealistic standards, but City Hall favored his crime plan. Chief Jorden was stiff, hell-bent on results. If it wasn't for Chance and Miles, Sgt. Neal's squad would have been the worst in the division. Besides Gatewood, Sgt. Neal had Joe Ellis and Bobby Zeat. Being in

Homicide for as long as Neal himself, both men were well seasoned. Gatewood, a female who stuck out from the others, was the newcomer. Having only been in the division for eighteen months, she had yet to meet the standards or expectations of her promotion, but it was mandatory all fresh meat be tested. He'd done all he could to redeem the detective; now she had to save herself.

"Neal," Capt. Dagger yelled out, walking towards the dazed sergeant.

"Hey, Captain," he replied without removing his eyes from the board.

Capt. Dagger stood next to him, staring at the numbers as well. He read the sergeant's mind. "Yes, yes, yes, those digits are ugly, but what is it to do when you're doing all you can?"

Sgt. Neal's focus bounced between the captain and the board. The scowl of a brow made the answer to Dagger's question self-explanatory. A concrete solution seemed hopeless. "Maybe we could use more manpower."

The captain rephrased it, "Or the power to make the men we have work harder. Each detective has to carry the weight of his own shield."

Sgt. Neal had to agree to disagree, "They're already

working their asses off, pulling doubles and triples. These detectives are passionate about solving murders and lowering the numbers. With every solved case, three more bodies drop... just a cycle that doesn't quit."

He gently bobbed his chin up and down, knowing exactly where Neal was coming from.

"This is all bullshit!"

Capt. Dagger felt hostility brewing within the sergeant. "What's bullshit?"

"Forget about it-"

The captain pried, "No, elaborate."

Sgt. Neal took advantage of the invitation, "I'm watching people around me fall apart. Most of the detectives in rotation have sacrificed everything, minus their limbs, to become a part of the solution. Some lost spouses to put the necessary time in that we're demanding. This makes them servants of burden, not love."

"In all due respect," Capt. Dagger spoke inconsiderately, "that's not my problem. If they picked the job, do the job. You're the only one I see complaining."

Sgt. Neal held his palms up as if instructed to freeze. "This is the reason I keep my trap shut."

"Why," inquired Capt. Dagger, leaning against the

board, "because we differ in opinion? You think the chief's too hard; I think he's not hard enough. But if you got a problem with how he does his job, take that up with him. Truth be told, everybody isn't cut out for this line of work. Many are called, chosen are few. Chief Jorden's system separates boys from men."

Sgt. Neal had to remember how much the albino's mind was whitewashed. His emotions were detached from the detectives who slaved each day, seeing them as machines rather than people. Since there was no helping him see the bigger picture, Sgt. Neal turned his sight back to the board.

"I know why you feel the way you do. It's not called compassion, no, not at all; it's called Christy Gatewood," said Capt. Dagger.

Sgt. Neal's lips shivered with disdain, but he showed discipline.

"What is it with you and this little girl, huh?"

The sergeant looked at him but refused to respond.

"I've given her the same chance and opportunity as everyone else. She weaseled her way in off of Raymond's rep, but how fair is that to the ones, yes, those same ones you just finished speaking of, who gave everything but a limb to be where they are today? Better yet, I can see if Gatewood was outstanding, carrying a championship belt as she done in those other divisions, but she's nothing like her old man. I could put that badge on a squirrel, bet it'll lock away more nuts."

Sgt. Neal couldn't help but ask, "Is there another reason, besides her poor job performance, why you're counting her out?"

"Nope, nothing more than what I mentioned," he coolly admitted.

"Since we're being honest, tell me," Sgt. Neal stared him straight in the pupils, "who tipped off Chance and Miles about the time limit I was ordered to give her?"

Capt. Dagger broke eye contact.

"Yeah, that's what I thought." The sergeant gave the man his back.

"So what, yes, I told them. No big deal. I answered your question... now answer mine. What is this relationship between you two?"

Sgt. Neal had nothing to hide. He expounded by muttering over a shoulder, "Let's just say me and her father shared some of the same loves, and, out of that love, I feel it's my duty to see her through."

The captain addressed the back of Sgt. Neal's lumpy head, "Well, she has a little over a day to show me something good, or you won't be burdened with that duty any longer. Got that?"

Pressed for no more rap, the sergeant stepped off.

BOOK TWENTY-TWO

Hot saliva drizzled down the sides of her breast. For some unfamiliar reason, realizing she wanted him just as bad as he wanted her, Christy lost the desire to scream for help, but she couldn't give in that easy. Hoping a lie would deter his actions, she said, "Please don't do this. I'm on my cycle."

He sucked her nipples with more force. Christy being on her period aroused him even more. To take her out of bounds, similar to the women he pulled over to sexually harass, was right up his perverted alley. Just to know Christy's vagina was bloody and out of service, not to mention wasn't his to have, those forbidden thoughts made Tony's meat double in size.

The nipple sucking turned Christy coy. He slowly worked his saliva-soaked hands down her stomach and over the mound of her sugar pot. As he toyed with its pubic fuzz, a defiant moan rolled off of her tongue.

"Like it, don't you?"

Although she yearned for more, her face showed disapproval.

"Stubborn aye? This will make you talk." He unhanded

her mound, clutching her crotch.

From what Christy felt, his fingers were about to go to work. Anticipation made her sigh. The fantasy of it was fine until his thumb grazed her pinkness, causing nervousness. "Okay, that's enough. Stop. Untie me," she demanded.

He gave her nipples a break. "Now you got a voice. Sorry, too late," he muttered, rubbing the mouth of her pussy.

"I said that's enough!"

"Shut the fuck up! You are no longer in control. This pussy is under my management."

She changed her tone, "Please stop. I'm not ready for this."

"It's sooooo goddamn tight. You should be ashamed of yourself."

The embarrassment made her want to crawl under a rock.

Tony misread her expression. Deciphering it as though she was about to scream, he quickly intercepted, "You better not do it!"

"You're taking this too far."

"You haven't seen anything yet." He forced Christy's legs up without warning, swiftly burying his face in her pussy.

She struggled to stop him, but the slithery spell of his tongue took control of her energy. Any urge to scream became an urge to yelp, and an urge to fight became an urge to surrender. This was a feeling Christy never experienced, a sensation that made her troubles vanish. When reading about Natosha's first sexual adventure, the way Troy handled her from the back, Christy assumed the experience was beautiful. The woman even found herself wishing she and Natosha could have switched places. But Natosha's book was closed, her supple limbs were presently open, and Tony was sucking on her clitoris with his vacuum-powered lips. If only he knew how much she enjoyed his abominable behavior. "...Oh ...My ...God," she moaned.

"You lied about your period," he mumbled, using his tongue to punish her.

More willing than woeful, Christy could only respond by groaning louder.

He secretly smirked as his oral assault violated her right to remain silent. Sticky sap oozed out of her virgin passage in creamy gobs, lugging a richness which called its sweet scent into account. Before that precious honey wasted, Tony lapped it up.

The pleasure made her eyes moist. After preserving herself to find the man of her dreams, only to have her sacredness degraded and disregarded in a single instance, that chiseled at her self-esteem. Tony gained access to a treasure he didn't deserve. As the boorish man cleaned up her vaginal leak, working his way back to the source of its spill, her mind was blown.

"Mmmmmmmmah," he kissed her pussy hole, and that's when the tongue-fucking started.

"Oooooooh," she cried out, feeling the thickness of his tongue penetrate her. He noisily ate until she felt an explosion looming. His tongue jabbed at her tunnel, causing her eyes to reel like a slot machine. An orgasm struck so violently that every part of her body locked. Once the spasms subsided, he released her legs, licking his way back up her belly. Christy was still breathing heavy when she heard the crackling of Tony's zipper. The sound snapped her back into reality. Again, she tried to push him up, this time exhausting herself in the struggle.

Tony knew, following the rape, he couldn't let her live. The cunnilingus was an incentive that influenced what he planned to do next. Desperation caused her to fight by squirming off the couch and onto the floor. She fought until ending up on her stomach, gown tightly coiled around her shoulders and abdomen. To terminate the skirmish, he shoved a knee into her back, pushing her face into the plush carpet, nearly suffocating the distraught woman.

"If you continue to fight, the end result won't be in your favor."

"Mmmmmmmm-mmmmmmmm," she bewailed, trying to catch her breath.

Turning her face to one side, Tony put his lips to her ear, "That was just a warning. Now breathe... breathe..."

She inhaled and exhaled as coached, submitting. If Christy gave him what he wanted, she prayed the disgraceful event would come to a fast end.

"No more resistance. Do I make myself clear?"

"Yes."

Christy's dad taught her that you never know a person until inviting them into your home. Anything can transpire behind closed doors. The outside world can't see through walls. She blamed herself for going against the golden rule.

"You're my little slut," he said, yanking her panties down. The flimsy cotton stopped at her ankles. Tony opened his trousers, sticking his well-endowed pipe between her soft ass cheeks.

She winced.

"Yeah, just like that," he mumbled as the length of his manhood melted into her spread. "I know a maiden when I see one. Don't think I didn't taste your sweet hymen. You're a virgin, aren't you?"

The detective was so focused on his swelling penis that she could only envision the impossibility of it fitting inside of her tiny portal.

"Speak!"

Christy cowered at the spike of his voice. His treacherous behavior made her emotional. The man was a psycho, one who already attempted to suffocate her. She blandly responded, "Yes. I've never had intercourse."

"Put more feeling into it when you're talking about my pussy! Who fucking virgin pussy is this?" he aggressively asked.

"Y-Y-Your v-virgin pussy," she stuttered.

That turned his dick into a stone.

"I'll be nice and give you a choice." He took the head of his banana and placed it at the door of her womb. "I can take your sweet cherry or stick it in your ass. Those are your two options. Speak!"

Christy didn't know what to say. She paused, thinking about how much she cherished her hymen. Once severed, it could never be restored. She didn't want to lose her cherry to a depraved individual; on the reverse, her rectum would ultimately tighten back up. To be sexed in either hole would hurt like hell. Feeling Tony about to shove himself right up her pussy, she blurted in shame, "My ass... my ass."

"Huh?" He slowly moistened the head with her wetness. "I didn't hear you. What was that?"

Christy repeated herself, "My ass.. put it in my ass." Her eyes closed to bucket the tears.

"First I suck your pussy, now you invite me to your asshole. Damn," he doused his shaft with spit, "you are my kind of woman." Wasting not another second, his log tore into her tightness.

"AAAAAH!" She twitched, trying to run.

He worked himself in and out of her moistness. "Stop moving. It'll loosen up." Tony then smacked Christy on the ass to relieve her tensed spine. Eventually his lustful taps made her subordinate. He licked on the back of her neck, pushing himself deeper inside.

"Ooooooh-mmmmmmuh," she moaned at a high pitch, hardly

enduring his drilling process. When the rectal elastic gave way, a numbness eased her anal muscle.

"Your asshole is so good. I can live in this until doomsday," said Tony, forcing himself nutts-deep. He gave Christy two fingers to pacify. The combination of her mouth and asshole drove him mad.

"Uuuuuuuuh-oooooh-ahhhhh," she sighed, slowly but surely welcoming the pleasure.

He closed his eyes, dicking her down at a love-making pace. It felt—*Kill her now! This is what we are called to do. You gave us your word*—so wonderful. The voice of **It** was in his head. Once **It**—*She is a demon like the rest. You must destroy her*—starts, there was no shut-off valve. Tony tried to exclude **It** by making Christy's dirt road the center of attention. The deeper he stroked—*We definitely can not allow her to bend our course. For what good is it to gain the world but lose your own soul?*—the voice got increasingly louder. It was correct, but he was stuck in a moment of bliss. Knowing he was about to kill Christy gave him an adrenaline rush. Tony stroked hard and fast.

Christy's asshole was now loose and horny. She never knew the pleasure of sex could feel so heavenly. To be introduced to it in such a forbidden fashion, it took her mind to a new zenith. How he fucked her, Christy wouldn't be interested in receiving it any other way.

Tony gritted—*Don't ignore me. It was her kind who put us in this situation*—his teeth, working his hips until sweat ran down his back.

"Tony... Tony... Shit! Fuck me!" she shouted, throwing her ass back. Christy's pussy was close to squirting.

While her outburst stunned him, her asshole clenched tightly. He eased his hands around her neck, peering down—*Yes! Yes! Yes! Choke! Choke! Choke! Choke!*—grunting like a gorilla.

Fireworks went off inside of Christy as she shouted, "I love it... I love it..." Cream flooded both holes. "From now on, it's yours."

That statement also—*Don't listen to her. She's a liar. Finish the harlot!*—took him by surprise. With all that he'd done in an attempt to break her spirit, the detective actually enjoyed it, which was rare. Thinking about other sadistic shit, she might readily accept, gave him the chills. In Tony's mind, without a doubt or contradiction, for her the worst was yet to come. He took his hands from around her neck. Christy continued to back—*What are you doing? Don't let her go. She's going to send you to prison.*

You're being stupid!—her ass up until he splattering her chocolate highway with steamy spoo.

She accepted every drop, turning to give him a juicy kiss. Their first sexual interaction was the bomb.

With the officer's lustful nature quenched, his mental faculties were slowly restored. The voice in his head said nothing else. It's funny how Christy never knew how close she came to death. As his penis deflated, he chose a reasonable explanation for his actions. Tony opened his mouth and said, "I love role playing. Did you enjoy it?"

She batted her eyes. "Being sodomized and bound against my will?"

He pulled his limp penis out of her.

"You come to my home and sex me without mutual consent. I can put you in jail for the rest of your life. Your conduct was inexcusable, an absolute crime."

He was about to grab her neck and squeeze.

"But I fucking loved it! You made me feel amazing. Needed that."

Realizing she wouldn't pursue the matter, he stopped in motion. Christy came close to dying twice had her response been otherwise.

Coming to terms with her own freaky inner woman was

just as embarrassing as what he'd done. It's weird what the mind was able to accept when exposed to a particular element of pleasure. As frightened as she was at the onset of his assault, Christy was now at ease. Suspecting him as a person of interest in Natosha's case, especially after revealing a savage side she didn't know, never crossed her mind.

Tony freed Christy's hands. "If I was too aggressive, I'm sorry. I truly didn't mean to impose my will on you."

With her asshole still on fire, she pulled her panties up. "That's the one thing I didn't like, so you got a lot of making up to do."

Running game, he fastened his trousers and reached for her palms. "I want you to be my girl. With you beside me, we're going to have some fun times."

She wanted to accept the offer but postponed her answer. "Let me think about it."

He kissed her palm. "You already agreed to being mine."

"Not me," she said, pointing to her private region.

He got the message and smiled.

Christy fixed her gown, moved her lips close to his, pressing her breast against his chest. "You will allow me to give you the cat on my time. That is how you make it up to me."

He took it with a grain of salt. "Okay, on your time."

"No pressure?"

"No pressure," he promised.

"Alright, I got to soak. Let me walk you to your car. We'll hang out again tomorrow." She hobbled to the closet and threw on a trench coat.

* * * *

"Will you take a look at this," uttered Chance. He and his partner were wooed to see Christy emerge from her building with a male in tow. They seen him come in earlier but mistook him for a tenant.

"So that's who he was coming to see. I was beginning to think she was a fish eater, but it seems she's not a vegetarian after all. Gatewood's splitting the pie with him and Neal, interesting," uttered Miles.

Chance studied the male, laboring to develop a potential profile. "Hold the mustard," the detective took a more in-depth look, "that dude is a uniform."

Mile's strained his eyes instead of grabbing the binoculars.

Trying to place the man's face with a name, Chance said, "I got it. He's one of the new guys at the Eastern District. Think about those uniforms who assisted us when we entered that house on Greenmount Avenue. It wasn't long ago."

"Oooooh, you mean when we arrested that Jamal Carter guy?"

"Riiight."

"Yeah, now I recall the face. He was the rookie officer who dropped his badge, almost lost the shit."

Chance built on the thought, "It would of been lost had I not picked it up."

The rookie's stupidity made both men shake their heads. The car got silent as they watched the couple stop at a Ford Windstar.

Miles asked, "What was his name?"

Chance nibbled on a fingernail. "I don't remember."

Miles carelessly relinquished the inquisition, saying, "Bump the damn name. It holds no weight."

"Hate when I get a brain freeze," said Chance, knocking on his own skull.

"Man never forgets; he just misplaces the thought. It'll come to us in time," uttered Miles, convinced.

They observed her give a kiss and return back into the building.

* * * *

Christy did feel guilt, but maybe that was a normal feeling after sex. Tony helped her realize that she was a woman before a detective; therefore, as a female, she had physical needs. She wondered if Tony could make a good husband, but it was too early to consider. Subsequent to soaking, her bowels suffered the discomfort of an aftershock. The pain of his penis caught up with her. All night, shifting in different sleeping positions, Christy couldn't seem to get it right. Luckily, her crises conceded an hour before it was time to prepare for another day in the field.

BOOK TWENTY-THREE

I constantly had ta convince mommy 'bout how important it was fa me ta attend church. Not sometime, every week. Told her it was Rose's church I felt most comfortable wit. When she asked why it was so necessary fa me ta go there, I said 'cause dem people were friendly and had a perfect understandin' of scripture. Yeah, I fibbed, but what if I told her Rose's church didn't really exist? Or told her dat dis was my only way of seein' or spendin' time wit Troy? She would of kept me home. But my church scam worked 'cause most weekends mommy cut me loose. Da only time she held me hostage was when there were chores 'round da house, so I always made sure da house was excellent before my time of departure. Since she gave my release papers on weekends, I'd call Troy and meet up. We'd begin every weekend goin' ta da park, readin' scripture ta each other. Den he'd take me ta his house. He lived wit his grandmova. She was a sweet lady. Neva cared 'bout me comin' ova ta spend da night. She even let us sleep in da same bed.

Troy was a gentleman when it came ta da Lord, but a

creature between da sheets. Since I neva denied him sex, da night's air would be filled wit constant, countless moans. Neva failed ta please me ta da fullest. We didn't use condoms. Truthfully, I was illiterate ta da dangers of gettin' screwed rawdog. Only knew it felt good. Had ta have him inside me, always. He wasn't insecure 'bout other guys. Told him he was da only male I'd eva accept in my heart. In turn, neva worried 'bout him and females, even though other girls called da house when I was there. He had my head in da clouds. Our love wasn't restricted ta just da earthly kind expressed through cards and gifts, hugs and kisses, or sexual gratification. Our love was God himself. He bestowed favor upon us.

At seventeen, I developed unusual symptoms. Started chuckin' up food, feelin' woozy and heavy. Thought it was da flu till I confided in Rose.

"Do you throw up a lot?" she asked.

"Yeah. Like most times when I wake up in da mornin'."

"When was ya last period?"

Dat took some thinkin' 'bout. "Hummmm, like two months now."

Rose murmured into da phone, "I ain't tryna scare you,

but it sound like you got a bun in the oven. I know you ain't let Troy hit you raw?"

I answered her question by lookin' at da ceilin'."

"Girrrrl, if you knocked up, gonna have to tell ya momma."

"Done bumped cha head," I said. "My mova would kill me, you, and da baby."

Her response came wit a chuckle, "What I got to do with that?"

"Stop playin'. I'm really afraid." My emotions were whisked.

"Then get an abortion."

"God would neva forgive me, neither would Troy. Plus, I'm still under age, so I'll need my mova's consent, I think. There has ta be a betta way."

"At least you should tell Troy. If you're pregnant with his child, he can be apart of ya decision making process. That's the fair thang to do. See what his ideas are, and go from there. All else fails, I want you to remember one word..."

"God save me?"

"That's three words, girl."

"Prayer?"

"No. Castor oil."

"Hey," I corrected her, "dat's two words."

"Two you better not forget," stated Rose, matter-of-factly.

Da castor oil idea didn't register, but what she said 'bout talkin' ta Troy did. So I took Rose's advice.

Da next weekend me and Troy hooked up and went ta his house. Da whole pregnant conversation was hard ta bring up. It was a step too big fa my small feet. Took a leap of faith, anywhoz.

"Troy, we need ta have a serious talk," I said as he was kissin' on me. We were inside da bathroom, and he had me against da sink.

"About what?" my love asked between kisses.

"Us and a possibility."

His expression was lost.

One at a time, stared into each eyeball, perhaps seekin' ta be rescued. "I might be pregnant."

"By who?"

Couldn't believe he asked dat. I removed his arms from 'round me. "What chu mean, by who? You my only lover. If I'm pregnant, it's your baby."

A brow battle came and went. "Wasn't saying it like that. We just never talked about having a family."

His sullen demeanor stabbed my heart. "Dat's somedin you should of thought 'bout before you started screwin' me without protection."

He grimaced. "Let's not start pointing fingers. You are just as much the blame. Do you even know if you're pregnant for sure?"

I sniveled tryna unscramble da facts. My voice lowered, "Well, haven't seen my bandit in two months."

Troy finally removed his heart from a coat pocket, reachin' ta console me. "Don't cry, baby. Before leaping to conclusions, we need to verify if you are or not. We can get one of those pregnancy tests from the Dollar Store."

I banged my fist against his chest. "Don't want no cheap dollar-store test. I need ta see a doctor!"

He stiffened. "We don't want no doctor in our business. You'll need insurance, with that comes ya name and social security number. Once they punch that information up, they'll know you're just a kid and contact your mother."

We stood divided on da matter, but his support was a

commodity dis situation couldn't do without. "I don't care. Been feelin' sick and dat's a thang I'm not used to. Peein' on a stick won't stop da dizziness."

"This can be sorted without a doctor."

My foot stomped da tile. "I need a professional opinion. It's not cha body goin' through changes. Why you takin' me on a marry-go-round?"

He slouched his shoulders in alinement wit mine. "Okay, we'll see a doctor. But instead of going to the hospital, I'll take you to the free clinic... that way you can give them a fake name, address, social, and age. You'll tell them you need a pregnancy test, nothing else. Once we find out the facts, we brainstorm to see what's next."

My man secured me wit a tight hug, and we discussed it no further.

Da followin' Monday I hooked school. Troy took me ta da free clinic on North Avenue. I gave dem my name wit a bogus age. Made up a social and used Rose's address. Da doctor called me ta da back, got nosy, took blood, and made me pee inna cup. After we finished, was sent back out ta da waitin' area. Troy held me fa reassurance. Da doctor came out an hour later and called me by number fa confidentiality purposes. I was privately seated inside her office.

She said, "You are pregnant."

I started cryin'.

She gave me a card. "Your other tests will take a couple of days to come back. When you return, the process will be simple. You walk in, hand this card to the receptionist, and we'll give you your lab results. It's an in-and-out thing."

I didn't feel da need da worry 'bout blood work or even mention it ta my baby's daddy.

She tapped my leg wit da affection of a woman who understood da struggle. "You got to dry your eyes and think about that new bundle of joy you're carrying. Be strong for your baby. Cheer up."

I wiped away some tears. "I neva been pregnant... don't know nothin' 'bout babies."

"Sweetheart, that's the chance you took when not using a contraceptive. You girls come in here all the time ill-prepared, exchanging your childhood for a moment of pleasure. You're a mother to be, so it's time to think like one."

"Where do I begin?"

"By following up with prenatal care. You don't want your baby unhealthy. That's for starters."

Though I had no plans on comin' back, took da card from da table. I shared da news wit Troy, and we went ta da park ta make plans.

Christy closed the diary. At the desk inside her cubical, she pondered on how close Tony came to impregnating her just last night. He sexed her without a jimmy. As freaky as it sounded, Christy was thankful he shot his load in her backside. But he still played around her vagina. All it took was pre-cum to get a female pregnant. Instead of troubling herself, she remained optimistic, for no fetus could grow inside of her bowels.

With her hours dwindling, work was put at the forefront. If anybody held presidential information on Natosha, Rose was the person Christy was anxious to interview. She hoped Rose could lead her to Troy.

Danielle was contacted and asked if she had a number to Natosha's besty. The mother explained how much she hated Rose and Stacy. Her underlining excuse was that the family mislead her daughter. Even still, Danielle had no workable number to provide but did give an address.

Christy jotted down the info, extending gratitude before hanging up. For what it was worth, a location supplied her with something to chase.

BOOK TWENTY-FOUR

With an arsenal of haunting thoughts beating at his temple, Tony woke up in another cold sweat, sofa soaked. Christy's face immediately came to mind. After disrespecting the woman with the sole purpose of killing her, he was unable to come to terms with the fact of leaving her alive. The liability of his actions could still cause a lengthy prison sentence. Christy wasn't some random, traffic-stop fling, she was a detective of all things. Akin to a traffic stop, he went hard on Christy and walked away like it never happened. Other women couldn't track him down, she could; moreover, the whole calvary could have come kicking his door off the hinges, but the house was quiet as it always been. Tony couldn't badger himself too much over not taking her life. He wasn't a murderer, didn't have the guts to outright kill anyone. But It was led by instinct, having no conscience. Tony's designated duty was to find those who were poison, guide It to them, and his work was done.

It was his fault It had come to exist. Staring in the eyes of a monster made him one. If Tony had the strength to pull himself away, he would have, but It would find him.

205

Thinking about eloping with the detective without repercussions, he knew such an idea was no more than a fairy tale. Above that, Christy would never place her future in his hands, not after what he'd done to her. He was incapable of slow walking into any substantial relationship so long as It was alive. Officer Bowles never fathomed killing It because, in a great sense, It was already dead.

As if It's telepathic attraction was impulsive, his vision was involuntarily swayed by the magnetic pull of the bedroom door.

"Toooonnneeey," It chanted his name. "Are we thinking about leaving us when there is no escape?"

How It grew with the innate ability to read his mind was astonishing, a true talent. "I wouldn't dare think of that," he perjured. "I'm indebted to us until our mission is complete."

"The words you speak are divorced from your heart."

Tony said what he thought was acceptable, "My heart is with us, not with those of this world."

"Then why isn't she dead?" It asked.

Tony stumbled over his next affirmation, "I-I couldn't r-reach her last night. Even tried to go p-past her house, but no one answered the bell."

It could smell the lie. The bedroom door savagely shook. "LET US OUT! HER BLOOD WILL BE SPILLED BY THE HANDS OF THE SAINTS INVESTED IN ME!"

"What's the rush?"

It's voice eerily shifted to a contralto, "It is written: No longer shall I dwell with you. For you are but flesh, enslaved by your carnal desires. This is why the earth is so contaminated. You have forsaken our duty to the Lord."

That statement came with an electrical effect. "If you wish to do this alone, go ahead. Fine!" Tony shouted. "You have no patience or faith in me."

"You have no faith in God."

"How can you say that when I've followed the Lord through your guidance? Shoulder-to-shoulder, we've armed ourselves and fought against evil."

"You've changed."

As tension roamed throughout the apartment, he begged, "Just give me one more chance to make this right. I'll succeed this time. I will not fail."

His pledge was clothed with passion. **It** understood that he was only a helper, not a do-it-yourself murderer; he needed training to grow into that role. Christy's death was his initiation. The creator was a forgiven God, so **It** exercised that forgiveness by granting him respite. "This is your final chance to show us you're still loyal to our calling."

"Thank you. Thank you," he said, heart trampling out of control.

"But this time you will bring us back her head as a brunt offering," **It** ordered. "The head will be used as a sacrifice for the sins you've committed. Afterwards, we will continue our duty to the Lord."

"I will bring her head back to you... that's my word."

With that, he moved from the confines of his sofa. Everything got quiet as though he was home alone the whole time.

BOOK TWENTY-FIVE

Stacy was exiting her yard when approached by a strange woman.

"Excuse me, ma'am, but I'm looking for Stacy or Rose," said Christy.

Visually suspicious, the mother withdrew a smirk before it settled. "I'm Stacy. Who are you?"

She did her rendition of badge flashing. "I'm Detective Gatewood, Baltimore Homicide. May I have a word with your daughter?"

The frowning of Stacy's face wrinkled the bridge of her broad nose. "What type of games you people playing?"

Christy didn't comprehend the response, and, obviously, Stacy didn't understand her request either. "Ma'am, I'm looking for your daughter."

"If you haven't found her by now, you guys aren't looking hard enough."

Christy stared at the caramel, evenly proportionate woman; she was speaking in riddles. "I'm not being sarcastic, but you're taking me in circles. So, let me say it like this, is Rose present?"

Arrows shot from her eyes. "No, she's missing."

The detective's jaw dropped. That wasn't the reply she expected. "Forgive my lack of knowledge, but this is new information to me. I have some questions. Can we step inside, or would you mind coming back to headquarters?"

Stacy hesitated, then refused. She wasn't for the shananigans. "Whatever you have to ask me, you can do it right here."

Christy couldn't force her downtown; she wasn't under arrest. In lieu of insisting without success, Christy played by Stacy's rules. "Okay, right here is perfect." She took a long swallow. "When did Rose go missing?"

"Two weeks ago."

"What is her full name?" Out came a pad.

"Rosemia White."

"R-O-S-E-M-I-A W-H-I-T-E?"

"Yes."

"When did you file the missing person's report?"

"Four days after she didn't come home."

Christy scowled. "Why so late?"

"I gave her time to return. Once she didn't, I got worried and contacted the police. I've been calling and calling, but all they keep saying is they haven't had any luck."

"When is the last time you spoke with her?"

"I was In Atlantic City the last we talked. She called and said her and a friend we're going to the movies."

"Did she give you the name of the friend or theater?"

"Neither," said Stacy, eyes weighty. "Rose is a grown woman. I don't get in her business or tell her what time to come home. For all I know, she might be with Natosha."

That speculation was unsettling. "Might you be referring to Natosha Little?"

More questions than answers, Stacy thought to herself. "Yes. That's who I assume she went to the movies with. I already informed the cops but didn't have Natosha's address or phone number."

The conversation blew a fuse. Remorsefully, Christy gave her a short news flash, "I'm sorry to tell you, but Natosha has passed away."

Shocked was an understatement. "When?"

"Two days ago."

The update was overwhelming. "What happened to her?"

"I believe she's the victim of a serial killer," uttered the detective, sparing the details.

The sound of that was unreal. "Then what about my Rose?"

She hiked her shoulders and let them drop.

Stacy lamented.

"Let's pray your daughter pops up. Hopefully, she knows what's going on and may be hiding herself from danger."

Measuring that flimsy logic, her head fell back against the wind. "Bullshit. Regardless, Rose would have still come home by now."

Christy interposed, "Probably under normal conditions, but different situations mandate different responses. We don't know."

On that last statement, they spontaneously arrived at the same mental terminal. Admitting not having a clue was the best thing the detective said yet.

"All I'm iterating is don't give up, neither will we. As of this second, no evidence points to your daughter hurt in anyway."

That was inspiring information. Stacy looked to the brightest cloud. "Thank you, Jesus."

"Nothing links her to Natosha's death."

"If nothing points to Rose, why are you here?" She cocked a brow.

"Because Rose is Natosha's best friend. I was hoping she could lead me to another friend who goes by the name of

Troy."

Her astute memory automatically reflected on the name.
"That boy is dead-"

"Huh?"

"Yup, committed suicide a few years ago. That's what I
heard... never met him face-to-face."

With Rose missing and Troy dead, Christy was sure the
Little's case would go cold. The only other male Natosha
mentioned was Lester. As far as she understood, Lester knew
Troy, so she questioned Stacy on his whereabouts.

The mother regretted the statement that followed,
"Lester also killed himself some months back. These young
men and these trends..."

Incredulously, Christy's spirit levitated out of her
body and peered down in third person. This string of
suicides really enlightened her to the magnitude of the
situation, it being much thicker than she imagined.
Natosha's death was just the first to open Pandora's box.
"Damn, I'm sorry to hear that. How'd he kill himself?"

"Found him hanging inside my sister's basement." Stacy
trembled. "I don't want to relive it. My daughter is out
there somewhere, finding her is all I'm focused on."

Suicide was becoming a word far too common in the

detective's vocabulary. Solving all these cases would take more than hours or days; it could take years to unravel a web so intricate.

"Ms. Detective, I have somewhere to be. But if you locate my daughter-"

"I'll be the first to contact you," Christy finished the sentence. "Thanks so much for your cooperation."

The two split.

Under a new strain, the detective headed home until deciding what to do next. Far as she was concerned, her career was done. Zero leads meant no suspects, and no suspects meant no arrests, which meant she would be cleaning out her cubicle. Christy let down the victims' families, her father included.

Chance and Miles finally won.

BOOK TWENTY-SIX

Though me nor Troy were financially stable, we agreed not only ta keep da baby but ta also keep it a secret. Didn't blame our unborn fa us bein' children ourselves. Had no right ta do dat. We surrendered ta da situation and trusted in God. A soft stomach made it easy ta hide da pregnancy from mommy. Keepin' my weekend adventures constant, dat gave Troy and I da proper quality time we needed. Troy was a doll in da beginnin', always rubbin' my tummy, massagin' my back and feet. I knew dat he loved me, but my reflection in his eyes wasn't da same. After while, our communication got shaky. I mean, we still met up on weekends, but our quality time transformed into 99% sex. No parks. No Bible studies. He justified his lustful fit by sayin' my pregnant vagina was good as church service; every time inside, he got da holy ghost. Dat sounded good and all, but somedin 'bout us was missin'. Wit his new eagerness ta be more physical than spiritual, he spoke less 'bout God and our baby. Whateva it was, da one thang I did know, our relationship went downhill.

Got worse when he went from spendin' time wit me ta

droppin' me off at his house and rollin' out. Sometimes he stayed out fa hours, other times he stayed out all night, leavin' me in his room alone. Female callers increased; dey even got sassy when I told dem he wasn't home. Approached him 'bout da disrespect, he'd scream in my face. I cried da God, askin' what I done wrong? What I do ta deserve dis pain?

My stomach and heart grew harder. Even at four months pregnant, still wasn't showin'. Though stress was eatin' me alive, Rose claimed I was carryin' my baby well. At dat time, it was a whole month since Troy touched me in any kind of way. He even stopped meetin' wit me. Found myself travelin' ta his house alone on weekends. Turned ta Rose in tears, tellin' her all I was goin' through.

She said, "That's how men are. They change when females get pregnant, but it's not on you," Rose embraced me like a big sista, "it's the baby that make them act that way. Subconsciously, he feels threatened. It's a territory thang us females will never understand."

Dat explained why my father disappeared. Dat wouldn't be me and Troy's story. "What can I do ta make him love me like he used ta?"

She squeezed me tighter. "My only solution is that word I told you not to forget. Remember?"

Thoughts jogged back. "Castor oil?"

"Very good," Rose uttered. "When you take it, you won't feel a thang. It's the cheapest abortion in the world."

Pondering it made me queasy. "I don't know 'bout dat. You sure dat's da right thang ta do?"

"I'm positive." Rose went in da kitchen and brought me a small bottle of oil. "Once the baby's gone, Troy will snap out of his evil trance. Watch what I say."

I journeyed ta Troy's house. Nothin' changed, was there by myself. His grandmova even left a note sayin' she wouldn't be back till da mornin'. Went in his room and prayed fa a long time. When calm eased ova me, knew dat was da Lord forgivin' me in advance fa what I was 'bout ta do. Once God assured me dat my sins were already washed away, I took da bottle of oil into da bathroom, locked myself inside, and sat on da toilet. Rubbin' my baby fa da last time, I chugged da bottle of oil and gagged at da taste. Everything seemed straight till my stomach tightened. What I underwent after dat was all but painless. Rose lied. First came da diarrhea, then contractions. It didn't take long fa a huge blood clot ta pass through my vagina. Da water in da toilet was dark. Floatin' in da middle was a mass of blood and veins. Dat's what remained of me and Troy's unborn. I got a plastic bag and scooped it out. Though took it upon myself ta kill our baby, he still had da right ta know, ta see it, ta be one wit it. Determined dat da baby, dead or alive, one way or da other, would be apart of his life, took da plastic bag downstairs ta prepare a spaghetti he'd always remember. Set da table wit candles and everything.

When Troy got in, rushed ta da door ta greet him. Instead of givin' me dat I-don't-want-ta-be-bothered look, he grabbed me, lips hoppin' all ova my face. Da trace was broken.

Told me how sorry he was fa treatin' me and da baby so bad. Claimed ta have talked wit God and promised thangs be betta. "I been under the weather about your pregnancy. It took me some soul searching to adjust, but I came to the conclusion that it's my duty to be the best father this world has to offer."

Dat was wonderful ta hear. I had Troy back ta myself. Told him I made dinner.

"Look at you, showing off." He rubbed my stomach. "What

did you make?"

"Spaghetti," I mumbled, pinnin' my vision ta his chest. Couldn't take back what was done. Havin' his love was my only objective. He pulled me ta da dinner table, smackin' my backside. Was told ta make him a nice plate of my homemade dish. As I heeded my man's request, da thought of our deceased child disturbed me. Rose influenced me ta take dat oil. Had I waited, everything would have naturally fell into place. Voved ta neva forgive Rose fa convincin' me ta make da biggest mistake of my life.

Was bleedin' too heavy ta lie by tellin' Troy I was still pregnant. If he had ta discover my deceitful deed on his own, was sure he'd have nothin' else ta do wit me. Da truth was always betta than a lie; it would set us free.

"What's the holdup on the grub. This is a special night for me, the first time I walk into a home-cooked meal, one made by your hands. Bae, you might be an okay chef, but you're making a poor waitress," he said, laughin'. Soon as I served his food, he dug right in. Sat next ta him, listenin' ta his tongue and lips smack in my ear. "Mmmmm-uump, delicious." Dat old glow in his eyes was restored. "You got these noodles extra meaty."

Troy noticed my quiet disposition. At any time he was bound ta inquire 'bout da baby, so I braced my mind, preparin' myself ta give him da absolute truth.

Halfway through his meal, he turned ta me and asked, "How's our little screamer?"

I closed my eyes and blurted, "You're eatin' it."

He stood from da table and spat what he was chewin'. Troy looked down at da plate as if starin' into a quasar. Thought his head was 'bout ta implode.

"Sorry," I whispered, standin', hurt and afraid.

"What the fuck have you done?"

He yanked me by da arm. "I killed it 'cause I thinked chu didn't want it, didn't want meeee. Dat fetus was comin' between us, so I fed it-"

"Don't want to fucking hear anymore." He pushed me towards da front door, shoutin', "You crazy bitch! Get the fuck out of my house. I don't ever want to see you again!"

His door slammin' in my face reminded me of Lester. There I was on his porch, shoeless, coatless, no sugar. Da night's brisk alerted me ta just how shameful I was. It was 2:00 am. With nowhere ta go, as usual, I turned ta Rose. Cold and shiverin', gave her a collect call from a phone booth. Bawlin', told her what happened. Didn't mention da ghetti but did say Troy put me out 'cause of da abortion.

She uttered, "Dang, that's messed up. But I'm happy you called. Soon as you left earlier, the Health Department came looking for a Keisha Little. They said it was a serious emergency. Did you give that free clinic my info?"

"I did, and Keisha Little was da fake name used. Your info was da only thang I could think 'bout when I was there. I'm sorry."

She dismissed my apology. "Ptite, I'm not mad, but they'll be back later today. I think you need to talk to those people to see what they want."

Dey probably was checkin' 'cause I didn't follow up wit prenatal care. Once I tell dem I lost da baby, dey'd leave me alone. Rose payed fa my cab ta her house.

When da evenin' came, just as dey promised, da Health Department showed up. Dey told me some shockin' news, and dat's when it hit me...

"That's when what hit you? Where the hell is the rest

of the Bible?" uttered Christy in anger, holding the last page in her hand. The diary had an inconclusive ending, leaving the detective wired up for more. The dead girl was a madwoman. To Christy, Natosha was just as dangerous as the perpetrator responsible for her death. The Bible led Christy nowhere. All that reading for nothing.

BOOK TWENTY-SEVEN

The detective was startled when her buzzer chimed. Unquestionably, someone must have had her humble abode mixed up. She spoke into the intercom, "Wrong apartment, try another button."

"Hey, Christy, it's Tony."

His voice stunned her. "What are you doing here?"

"My bad for the unexpected pop up, but I really need to holler at you. It's important," he said, rashly.

She was confused. "How'd you know I was home?"

"Your car is out here, dah."

"Tony, this is really bad timing. I'm totally busy," Christy proclaimed, wallowing in her own misery.

He wouldn't be deterred. "Look, feel awful about last night. I want to talk a few things over with you, make sure we're seeing eye-to-eye."

"It's no hard feelings... but I'm busy-"

"And I'm on duty. It won't take long. Can you buzz me up, please."

He sounded so pitiful through the speaker. She had doubts but challenged her own intuition. Postponing her better judgment, she buzzed him in. Taking caution, Christy fastened her door latch, restricting the entrance to just far as the chain would allow; she wasn't in the mood to be alone with him.

Tony raced up each step, disappointed to see the door only cracked. "Let me in."

"No. Holler at me from right there."

"I wasn't expecting to speak with you through a doorway. For all this, we could have talked over the phone."

She agreed by saying, "If my cell wasn't off and on the charger, we could have."

"Christy," he panted, "I made a mistake last night. Even though it brought us closer, I take full responsibility for the aftermath... mind, body, and soul. But we're bonded."

"I'm not too sure about that. Being caught in the moment, I may have said some things I didn't mean. This is a new day," she exclaimed, leaving last night in the past.

He petitioned, "Lying is not the way to establish trust."

"Neither is rape."

"I'm sorry for what I've done, but," he moved his lips between the crack, "it's so hard to control myself when around you. I never seen a rainbow so beautiful."

She was flattered but refrained from smiling. "Without trust, promises are shattered; without promise, there is no future."

"But we can have a future. Right now, today, I'm willing to love you forever."

Christy blushed, watching him descend to one knee.

"Will you marry me?"

His proposal made her heart plunge. This was a noble way to correct his wrongs. She was speechless, "I-I-I..."

"I know you want to be happy, me too, everybody does. Give me a chance to live up to your standards. I won't disappoint you," said Tony, using manipulation to get the door unlocked.

"I don't know what to say."

His expression was harmless. "Don't say anything, just open up."

Impaired by deceit, she gave in, closing the door to fumble with the lock. By the time Christy released the latch, she opened the door to Tony standing. Expeditiously crossing her threshold, his heat-seeking tongue found her mouth. As much as he tried to conceal lust, his sexual craving wore bold letters.

Christy spoke honestly, "I don't know if I can accept your proposal. We don't know much about each other. Things like that take time."

He stared, a wry smile.

A weird look in his eyes made her defenses go up.

"Christy, Christy, Christy," that wry smile transformed to a straight face, "all we got is time, so stop making excuses."

He stuck his tongue back in her mouth, this time so deep she almost choked. The detective thought of it as the kiss of death. It made her uncomfortable. Tony's next move was random, sticking his hand down her jeans, palming her ass.

"Give it to me."

Christy squirmed out of his grip. Resisting fear, she stated, "You can't be serious. What a contradiction."

Tony debated whether to kill her now or wait.

Seeing that he was plotting, she took a full step back. "Listen up, I will not be disrespected, violated, pushed to the floor like trash, or maliciously fucked up the ass. I'm a whole woman, and you will treat me with some respect and dignity in my home."

"None of that was on my mind, but since you brought it

up," he stepped closer, inhabiting the spot where she recently stood, "I'll do to you what I damn well please."

Convinced that Tony was on some freak shit, she tried to entice his lust in order to get near her side arm, which was in the bedroom. "Let's go to the back. There you can have your way in a respectful manner. I'd rather be on my bed, not floor."

Taking his mind off of murder for a second, her suggestion was understandable. "See, I knew you'd come around."

Christy caught a side view of her phone on the kitchen counter.

Tony followed her peripheral and said, "You won't be needing that."

Elevating Christy off of her feet in a vicious, backbreaking hug, it was so painful she kicked and punched. "Let me go!"

"Yeah, keep fighting. That's how I like it."

"Thought you'd make it up to me by waiting. You promised," she appealed.

"Promises are made to be shattered." He carried Christy into the bedroom and slammed her upon the mattress like a pro wrestler.

She reached across the bed to the location of her holster, but was grabbed by the waistline. "Stop it!"

With her holster hidden from his line of sight, not thinking she was going for a gun, he took it as if she was trying to retreat. "You know where all this running got you the last time."

Being pulled back, Christy clawed at the bed, peeling off the sheets. He yanked so hard from behind that it popped the front button of her jeans. That quick, back on her stomach, pants droopy, he straddled her from the rear.

Unbuckling his service belt, gun still attached, Tony whipped out his penis like a pocketknife. "Stay still."

She whimpered. "I shouldn't have let you in my house."

"Should'a, could'a, would'a," he mocked, holding her down.

"I'm begging you not to do this-"

Her plea fell upon deaf ears. "Shut your mouth. We both know you like it." Tony nearly ripped her panties getting them down.

"I'm still sore," she muttered.

"Don't worry. Your asshole is safe. I want this cherry."

"No! Tony! No!"

He jammed a finger into her pink tunnel so fast that Christy's hymen almost popped.

"Oaaaaaaauuch! Let me up, please. I don't want pregnancy!"

Lust struck, his mind wavered not. "I got a rubber around here somewhere."

At least, minus what she was about to withstand, that was a relief, Christy thought.

Tony tapped a pocket with his free hand. "Ooops, I'm fresh out."

"Think twice before you do this."

He giggled like a devious child, lathering his meat with her slippery juices. Without any compassion, he entered her with so much force that his right foot kicked Christy's dresser, fragmenting the frame of her family photo as it flew against a wall.

"Owwwwwwww-uhhhhhh," Christy wailed in pain.

"AARRRRRAHHH," he bemoaned, tearing into her unchartered guts.

The agony of being so roughly penetrated was torturous, but her womb swallowed every painful inch of Tony's mammoth. "Pleeeease goooo eeeeasy."

Ignoring her, he continued to stroke, pushing himself

to the limit. "ARRRRGH-RRRRAAH!"

"Oooooooh-aaaahhhhhhh! It's so deep!"

"Say my name!" he ordered, boxing her tender cervix.

Christy quickly shouted out, "TONY! TONY! TONY! OOOOOOH, TONY!" Her tight muscles loosened with every thrust.

When the tenseness withered, he slowed down his strokes, concentrating on her vaginal walls. "Give it to me. It's mine."

"Wooooooooh," she sighed, becoming more sensual.

"All this good pussy... it's amazing."

The rotation of his hips had her pie in a blender. It was something about being dominated that set her pilot ablaze. "Tony, daaaammn, you fucking the shit out of me."

He pumped even slower, caressing her body. Though being murdered by his paws was unavoidable, Tony momentarily stored those thoughts in the back of his mind. "You like the way I'm packing this pussy?"

"Yeeeess, it's the best."

He mumbled in her ear, "You're so wet, hot, and tight."

His whip appeal made her weak, helpless, and submissive. She lost sight of being a detective altogether; in fact, his sexual conjuration reduced her badge to scrap metal. He gave her a strong hour from the back. Under his lustful rule, she reached multiple orgasms. Suddenly, he jerked and started pumping erratically. She knew what that meant. "DOOOOOONNN'T CUUUUMMM INNNN MEEEEEE!"

"AAIEEEEEEEE-AAGGGGH-HRRRRN," he howled, withdrawing himself, splattering his load on the small of her back. The hot petroleum stayed in place. "That's the best pussy I ever had."

Hypnotized, her body went limp. Christy didn't know how to compute what had just happened. She was literally busted wide open, blood seeping from between her legs. "Your dick is the truth."

Tony looked down at the blood, taking it as a sign that it was time to murder her, though he couldn't do it without first motivating himself.

As he stood to pull up his uniform pants, Christy was surprised to see blood. She asked in a hushed tone, "Is that blood coming from me?"

"Yeah," he responded, cockily, "but don't stress yourself. That's what happens when you lose your cherry."

"No," she revolted, "don't get that on my carpet. Go to the bathroom. I'll meet you there."

He never seen a woman get raped and act normal as she

did. Turned out or not, play time was over. Officer Bowles planned on washing in the bathroom, that giving him a minute to tutor himself, return, and kill her. Decapitation would be the hardest part, but, even if he had to close his eyes and cut it off, her head was coming with him.

Sitting up in the bed, she watched Tony leave the room. Disgusted, the mess under Christy's butt paused her for an instance. Staying in place, Christy wrestled with the reality of no longer being a virgin. Moving a blanket away from the blood, she came across a receipt that must have fallen from Tony's pocket. Ropes, razors, and a box cutter were the purchased items on the invoice. Scribbled on the back was Linda's name and home address.

The words of Rodney hit her... *"Lin was upset tha last we spoke. She said some asshole cop pulled her over and was real touchy feely."* Christy thought about the bogus name tag at the restaurant. He was at Natosha's scene and also, apparently, interacted with Linda. How strange were those odds? That got the wheels spinning in her head. That's when the picture came together: **TONY WAS THE SUICIDE MURDERER!** Preparing herself for a real confrontation, the detective retrieved her gun and took position.

BOOK TWENTY-EIGHT

Miles' phone rung, and the number was from headquarters.

"Answer the damn thing," said Chance, annoyed as the result of sleep deprivation.

"After four rings, it makes us look busy. Relax." He put it on specker, "Detective Miles."

"Detective!" Sgt. Neal shouted into the phone.

Miles made a funny face at his partner. "I'm here."

"What's your twenty?"

"Babysitting at Gatewood's."

"Great," Sgt. Neal gasped, "I been trying to call her but can't get through. Anyway, a homicide she's working, Linda Foreman, some prints were pull off of the victim's ID. It came back to match a Troy Blue; the same prints also crosshatched a Tony Bowles."

"Bowles, Bowles, Bowles..." Chance inaudibly whispered, wondering why the name sounded so familiar.

Sgt. Neal continued, "Troy Blue has been linked to a string of crimes. This coward, according to the Health Department, is responsible for infecting several females with HIV. He's managed to change his identity, which allowed him to pass a successful background check. This guy is one of our own. As I speak, we're drafting a warrant for his arrest."

Chance clicked his fingers. "That's it."

"What?" asked Miles.

"The rookie's name I couldn't remember, Bowles... Tony Bowles."

Forgetting the sergeant was still on the line, Miles jumped out of the car. "Goddamnit, that guy is in there with her now."

Chance also hopped out, weapon drawn. "We got to get inside and see what apartment belongs to Gatewood."

Miles radioed for all available units to assist them at that location.

* * * *

When Tony reentered Christy's room, he was greeted by the nose of her 9 mm. "Put your hands up, and don't make me repeat myself," she ordered.

He gave an unsettled look. "I thought we were on good terms?"

"This isn't a game. You're about to get shot." Her

234

finger etched closer to the trigger.

He eased his hands up, saying, "What are you arresting me for, rape?"

"That and murder."

"The only thing I murdered was your pussy."

"Natosha Little, Linda foreman, and Brenda Webb... you murder their pussy's, too?"

Hearing that sequence of names, specially coming from Christy, was worst than being shot. Battling anxiety, Tony snickered, "You have no idea what you're talking about. Where's the evidence?"

"You purchased a box cutter," she waved the receipt, "planted it on Linda Foreman to make it look like a suicide, that was after you pulled her over. You killed Natosha Little, murdering Brenda Webb as a cover up. Thought you'd get away with killing those innocent females, didn't you?"

His eyes spoke, indecisively saying nothing. Christy had him by the balls, and there wasn't a thing he could do about it. The only option out was the service weapon plugged into the holster on his waist. He had to find a way to go for it.

[BUZZZZZZ! BUUZZZZZZ! BUZZZZZZZZZZZZZ!]

They both heard the bell. Christy didn't know who it was but used it against him. "You hear that? It's called backup. We can do this the easy or hard way. It's up to you."

Sirens echoed outside.

The bitter taste of defeat made him jittery. "Detective, you must listen, it wasn't me. It killed those women, made it look like suicides so It could remain undetected."

"It who? It what," she asked, bewildered.

"Natosha... she made me do it. She's fucking crazy!"

That statement exposed how looney and delusional he really was. "No, you're crazy. Natosha is dead! I seen her for myself. I'm the one investigating that case. Did you forget? As far as I'm concerned, you're It!"

The front door blasted open, and her name was shouted, "Gatewood! This is Detective Miles! The man you're with is an imposter, a fugitive! We've come to arrest him! Where are you?"

"I'm back here," Christy yelled, hearing footsteps. She kept her gun trained on Tony.

His nightmares finally came into fruition. He told It that this time would come. But dying in the process of doing God's will, that was the only thought that provided a sense of peace. A psychotic grin crept across his face, bringing him at one with self. As Detective Miles entered the bedroom, at the speed of light, Tony unholstered his own weapon. A millisecond before Christy could discharge her 9 mm., Tony put the gun in his mouth and pulled the trigger.

[BOOOOOOOM!]

BOOK TWENTY-NINE

After the crime scene was processed, as all three observed the corpse being carried away, Christy stood alongside Capt. Dagger and Sgt. Neal. The facts of his true identity and medical history had already been discussed with her. She now knew Tony and Troy were one in the same. He infected Natosha with HIV, and that's the reason why the Health Department wanted to speak with her. Since the deceased had unprotected sex with Christy, chances were she also contracted the deadly virus. Natosha probably lost her life in order for him to keep his medical history classified. He blamed his murderous behavior on **It**, attaching **It** to Natosha. He missed and loved the girl so much that his twisted mind rejected the fact that she was dead. The whole time Christy was reaching out to find the suspect, the fugitive was right before her eyes.

"I'll give it to you, Detective," Capt. Dagger patted her on the shoulder, "you did it big this time. You've closed four cases, including the suspect, in less than forty-eight hours. The good thing is you stopped a serial killer before the FBI had a chance to get a whiff. If that doesn't sound like a detective who can stand on her own," he bobbed his head, "then I'll be a monkey's uncle. Homicide is where you belong. Forget about the transfer."

The detective gave a triumphant smiled, "I appreciate that."

"I'll leave so you can get this place cleaned up," said Capt. Dagger, excusing himself.

Sgt. Neal picked up where the captain left off, "Yes, congratulations for doing such an outstanding job."

She responded with two syllables, "Checkmate."

"You finally mastered the game," he confirmed. "I hope you know I had your back the whole time. I believed in you the same way I had faith in your father. If he was still alive, today would be that day he'd be proud of you."

"Dad once told me that I'd make a difference in the world, and this day is the one he foresaw."

"He's watching over you in heaven; I'm watching over you on earth. Believe it or not, I look at you like my own daughter."

"That's nice to hear," she responded, giving him a hug. "Thank you for everything."

He savored the hug until it was over. "This is a lot of blood to clean up. I'll stay and help if you like-"

"No," she refused, "I'm fine. This place will be back

in shape in no time."

"Fair enough, I'll see you at the office," uttered Sgt. Neal, turning to help himself to the front door.

Soon as she heard it slam, Christy crumbled into tears. Only she knew how Troy sexually assaulted her while knowing he was infected with HIV. His quest was not to die alone, so he tried to take as many with him as possible. Christy wished he died by her gun, but suicide came back to haunt him. He passed away by the same fate he inflicted on others.

Christy cried until she was out of tears. Now came the time to get her apartment, as well as her life, back in order. She got a big bucket of water and bleach to begin her cleaning assignment. She first scrubbed away the blood and brains, disinfecting the whole room. The mattress was spoiled with new sheets; the old ones were stuffed in a bag to be washed. The cleaner the room got, the better the detective started to feel. She observed her family photo facedown, halfway under the bed. Broken glass surrounded the frame. As it was turned over, she noticed a few smaller photos taped to the back of the original. She stood with the broken frame, peeling off the tape to turn the pictures around. What Christy saw was addling: One photo was of Sgt.

Neal and her mom, Christina, kissing by a Christmas tree. A second photo was of the two cuddled in the nude.

Christy figured that was the reason why her dad started drinking, and maybe Rodney was correct about her father's death not being some random act of violence. This is what he was onto, and chances were Neal knew it. Though the photo's were evidence of a love affair, they lacked proof that the sergeant had a hand in her father's demise. The pictures were held as her new trump card.

Once the apartment was thoroughly cleaned, Christy went to do laundry. On the way to the laundry mat, she picked up Rodney a fifty-dollar money order. Since she wasn't going to ask another cop for an underhanded favor, sending him a little cash was the least she could do. The detective had enough of dirty cops, but, with the pictures she just discovered, there was a feeling that she would need Rodney's help again.

As Christy placed the money order inside the mailbox, her cell phone vibrated. She answered without recognizing the number, "Hello, Gatewood speaking."

"Detective Gatewood, this is Zozock Fatiu, Chief Medical Examiner at the morgue. I think we have a problem."

"In reference to?"

"It's concerning a body that was registered here a few days ago." He sniffed as if having a cold. "A female by the name of Natosha Little."

Recalling the frightening dream she had of Natosha at her apartment, in a frolic tone, Christy asked, "What... did her body get up and walk away?"

He spoke with zero humor, "Not at all. First the corpse has to be here to get up and walk out."

Christy paused en route to the car. "What are you saying, Mr. Fatiu?"

"It was difficult to identify the corpse; however, in partnership with a forensic buddy of mine, we were able to pull a small fraction of a thumb print."

"And what did you come up with?" Christy almost held her breath awaiting for the medical examiner to respond.

"Well," he spoke softer than a man should, "it came back a match for a Rosemia White. As unfortunate as it remains, the irony of it all, I'm proud to announce that Natosha's mom and dad can sleep comfortable at the fact of knowing their daughter is still alive."

Detective Gatewood went completely numb, phone falling to the hard concrete. Just when she thought the ride was over... it was only the beginning. Natosha was **IT!**

BOOK THIRTY

At Druid Hill Park, with a Bible sprawled across her lap, a female watched as children indulged in recreation. Inhaling a fresh scent of the grass-covered land, exhaling death, her pen moved with divine inspiration.

A small girl broke away from a play group, wandering over to a bench. She asked, "Are you readin' 'bout God?"

Natosha closed her Bible and smiled. "In fact, I am reading about God. Have you ever seen him?"

"Nope," the baby girl responded.

"I've seen him, and he's beautiful." Natosha's eyes sparkled with delight. "Would you like to see him if you could?"

"Umm-hummm." The child's head went up and down.

"Let me show you." She took the girl by the hand. Before anyone knew what was happening, the child was gone... never to be seen again.

The END?

A Message From The Autor

As an incarcerated writer, I transformed my cell into a classroom. Prison is a unique institution, one that should be used for self mastery. In this concentration college, its tuition comes with free room and board, also limited distractions. It welcomes no children or significant others. Sexual relationships are prohibited, which is more of a blessing than a curse. Maintaining abstinence helps to conquer the body, and every victory over self gives added strength.

Prison is a relative term: To the disadvantaged, prison is poverty; to a paraplegic, prison is a wheelchair; to a roach, it's a web; to a prisoner, it's a cell. In all reality, prison is only that which one accepts as such, a concept that restricts us from mental liberation. No matter the state of confinement, being it physical or spiritual, free your mind because possibilities are limitless. You'll succeed in your own recipe so long as failure is omitted as an ingredient. Time is a currency that can't be refunded. Spend it wisely. Invest every second (nickel), minute (dime), and hour (dollar) in your craft to achieve maximum success.

I thank Allah for my many long days and lonely nights, for affording me another moment to live out my purpose as a writer. I'm not here to change the game, only to man the torch. I write for the unborn who'll someday hold one of my books and gain inspiration to perpetuate this literary culture. Suicide Bible is just one of numerous titles. In-sha-allah, my fan base will hear a lot more from me. The best is yet to come!

Thank you for your time and support. For questions and comments, the following is my current mailing address:

Angelo Barnes #443697/1535732

P.O. Box 700

Jessup, Maryland 20794

Printed in the United States
by Baker & Taylor Publisher Services